Simeon Ford, Moses F. Sweetser

How to know New York City

A serviceable and trustworthy guide, having its starting point at the Grand Union

Hotel, just across the street from the Grand Central depot. Eleventh Edition

Simeon Ford, Moses F. Sweetser

How to know New York City
A serviceable and trustworthy guide, having its starting point at the Grand Union Hotel, just across the street from the Grand Central depot. Eleventh Edition

ISBN/EAN: 9783337255626

Printed in Europe, USA, Canada, Australia, Japan

Cover: Foto ©Andreas Hilbeck / pixelio.de

More available books at **www.hansebooks.com**

REVISED TO JANUARY 1, 1895.   WITH MAP

HOW TO KNOW

NEW YORK CITY

A SERVICEABLE AND TRUSTWORTHY GUIDE, HAVING ITS STARTING
POINT AT THE GRAND UNION HOTEL, JUST ACROSS THE
STREET FROM THE GRAND CENTRAL DEPOT

BY

M. F. SWEETSER AND SIMEON FORD

ELEVENTH EDITION

NEW YORK
PRESS OF J. J. LITTLE & CO
10 to 20 ASTOR PLACE
1895

A CORNER IN THE READING-ROOM OF THE GRAND UNION HOTEL.

HOW TO KNOW NEW YORK.

THE above picture represents a hotel-clerk, in the act of answering a question. From his bland expression, you would not suppose that he had been pretty steadily answering questions from his youth up, and has probably answered this very question upwards of a million times; but such is the case. A good hotel-clerk must be a walking encyclopædia, directory, railway, steamship, and postal guide, and, in short, a universal fountain of knowledge and information. No man is more maligned than the hotel-clerk. In current fiction he is de-scribed as a haughty and unapproachable despot, who, intrenched

behind a large diamond shirt-stud, superciliously assigns trembling
travellers to remote and cheerless chambers. As a matter of fact,
he is usually the most good-natured and accommodating of mortals.
Were he not of a serene and placid nature, he would long since have
decorated a cemetery. He is expected to be pleasant under the most
trying circumstances; to remember everybody by name, and all their
peculiarities and eccentricities; to give every one the best room in the
house; to laugh at every humorous anecdote related to him, no matter
how antique; and to lend a sympathetic ear to every traveller who is
in distress, or imagines that he is. For the aid of the stranger first
visiting New York, this modest work is prepared. It is not issued
for the benefit of the hotel-clerk (who still stands ready to answer any
and all questions), but to put before the visitor, clearly and briefly,
information which is likely to be of service to him.

It is hoped, too, that it may be the means of further calling to the
attention of the travelling public, the advantages offered by the Grand
Union Hotel, which, in brief, are as follows: It is just across the
street from the Grand Central Depot, to and from which baggage of
guests is taken free. Its location is convenient, street-cars and elevated roads passing its doors, to all points. It is conducted on the
European plan, and comfortable and well-furnished rooms may be
obtained at prices ranging from $1 to $5 per day. The *cuisine* is
first-class, and the prices are very moderate. It has a very large
patronage, and guests can live well at the Grand Union for less money
than at any other first-class hotel in New-York City.

Take Your Time. — New-Yorkers conduct business as though life
were fleeting. Go down town and watch the men in the streets! Every
one seems in a desperate hurry; and the visitor, without realizing it,
is apt to become imbued with the all-pervading hurry and scurry, and
finds himself rushing and elbowing his way through the crowd. This
haste is a characteristic of New-Yorkers, and the traveller who wishes
to see the city well must avoid their example. He must go slow, and
enjoy what he sees. Nothing is more fatiguing than sight-seeing.

Put up comfortably at the *Grand Union Hotel,* and don't try to see
every thing in a day.

NEW-YORK CITY.

New York is the chief city of America in wealth and population, and is second only to London as a financial and commercial centre of the world. Its population is about 1,801,000, one-third of whom are of foreign birth — mainly Irish and German. It covers over 27,000 acres of ground, and is about sixteen miles long, and from one-half to four and one-half miles wide. It is the main seaport of the United States. Upwards of 30,000 vessels annually arrive and depart from it. It is the great gateway for immigrants coming to this country. In one year 476,086 were landed at Castle Garden. It is the foremost manufacturing city of the United States, Philadelphia being the only city which approaches it in this field. According to the census of 1890, the value of articles manufactured in the city during the year was $777,222,721. There are 25,403 factories, one-fourth of which are devoted to clothing, cigars, furniture, and printing. 3,639 clothing establishments produce $87,533,259 worth of goods yearly ; 1,166 printing and publishing houses turn out $54,488,179 worth a year ; 1,282 factories produce $33,452,430 worth of cigars ; and 563 shops make $15,661,491 worth of furniture. It is the Mecca toward which Americans journey, and the city where millionnaires, no matter where they may have acquired their wealth, come to live, and to spend their money. No other American city furnishes such manifold and un-bounded opportunities for disposing of superfluous wealth. Fifth and Madison Avenues are lined with palaces, peopled by men grown rich in other places. No city of the world has such magnificent dwellings, such prodigious commercial and public buildings, such interesting shops and stores. It is the city which every American longs at some time to see; and we will remark, with the modesty which is always characteristic of hotel-men, that the proper place for them to stop while seeing it, is at the Grand Union Hotel, opposite the Grand Central Depot. Aside from the so-called objects of interest, such as museums, parks, theatres, etc., the visitor will find in the public streets, and the people who throng them, an endless source of amusement and interest. New York is eminently a cosmopolitan city. Its population is made up of the people of every clime. In different parts of the city, there are colonies made up almost exclusively of foreigners.

"*Germany.*"—East of Second Avenue, and extending from Houston up to 14th Street, is a region called "Germany." Here one can study the Teutonic character, without the danger of an ocean-voyage. Signs are in German; the German language is spoken; lager-beer is the prevailing fluid; and, with the aid of a lively imagination, the visitor may fancy himself in the " Vaterland."

"*Italy*" is the name given to another part of the city, centring about the Five Points. Here children of sunny Italy may be found disporting themselves in great numbers, many of them still wearing their picturesque native costumes, and speaking no language but their own. They are peaceable, industrious, and sober citizens. Cleanliness, however, is not their specialty. The entire Italian population do not, as is commonly supposed, devote themselves to the manipulation of the hand-organ, or the sale of the cheap (yet nutritious) peanut. Many of them are waiters, rag-pickers, and street-laborers; and among the higher class, there are music-teachers, literary men, professors of languages, etc.

"*China.*"—The traveller desirous of viewing the almond-eyed Celestial in his full glory, should visit Mott Street on a Sunday night. Here ' John " may be seen, arrayed in all the splendor of Chinese apparel, his shirt-tails picturesquely worn outside, and his pigtail floating in the breeze, indulging in the relaxation to which his six days and nights of uninterrupted labor at the great Chinese national industry, laundrying, has so richly entitled him. Here he smokes his opium, plays his mysterious games of chance, worships in his peculiar way, and minds his own business with a steadfastness of purpose which is worthy of emulation by people claiming to be more advanced in civilization than he. Among the women of the lower class of Irish and Italians, " John " is looked upon as a prize in the matrimonial market He makes a good husband ; for he not only provides the funds for the maintenance of the family, but, at odd times, tends the baby, and does all the housework, washing, sewing, etc. His dispo· sition is peaceful; but when disputes arise, as they will in the best-regulated households, his pigtail, always within easy reach, offers the partner of his joys and sorrows a convenient medium for the vindication of her outraged feelings. When a robust female attaches herself to the end of " John's " pigtail, he generally yields the point in dispute, without further argument. In this outlandish quarter, you may buy, at the Chinese groceries, the luscious Langi nuts, and the leathery abalene, which looks and tastes like ancient boot-heels. Here the Chinese Freemasons hold their mystic lodges; and quaint New-Year's festivities enliven the scene ; and devout Celestials worship their strange gods, in the joss-house at 202 Park Row.

" *Africa.*" — Thompson Street, just north of Canal Street, is sometimes called by this name, by reason of its being almost exclusively occupied by the dusky Ethiopian. The negroes are industrious and peaceable citizens, good-natured and happy under all circumstances. It is a popular superstition, that the negro, on the slightest pretext, " pulls a razor," and proceeds to carve every one in his vicinity, revelling meanwhile in gore. The writer, however, has several times penetrated the jungles of Thompson Street, and has thus far escaped either mutilation or sudden death.

" *Judæa* " is near the east end of Canal Street, around Ludlow Street and East Broadway, where this wondrously preserved Semitic people are found in great numbers. There are over 100,000 Hebrews in New York, with about 40 synagogues, and twice as many smaller shrines, and a score of societies of charity. They form one-tenth of the city's population, but less than one-hundredth of its criminals come from their number. There are 42 Hebrew millionaires in New

York ; their estates ranging from Max Weil's $8,000,000, downward through the Seligmans and Wormsers and Bernheimers, to the score of one-million-dollar men.

Population.—The census (1890) gives New York 1,801,000 inhabitants, of whom 727,629 were American born, and 639,943 of foreign birth.   Of these, 198,595 were from Ireland, 35,907 from England, 11,242 from Scotland, and 965 from Wales.   Germany contributed 201,723 ; Italy, 39,951 ; France, 10,535 ; Russia, 48,790 ; Spain, 887. There were 17,937 New-Jersey-born New-Yorkers ; 11,055 from Pennsylvania ; 10,589 from Massachusetts.

Buildings, etc.—There are over 100,000 buildings in the city, 70,000 of which are below 59th Street.   25,000 of them are used for business purposes, and 77,000 for dwellings.   140 of the buildings are fire-proof.   There are 306 piers, and 144 bridges.

Districts.—The city has 35 assembly districts, 9 State senatorial districts, and 9 Congressional districts.   There are 1,100 polling-places and registries.

Fire-Department consists of 84 steam fire-engines, 3 water-towers, 38 hook-and-ladder trucks, a life-saving corps, 1,080 miles of fire-alarm telegraph, 980 alarm-boxes, 350 horses, and 1,000 men.   It costs $2,300,000 a year.   There are 73 companies, making 12 battalions, each under a chief of battalion.

Police-Department has 36 precincts and station-houses, 75 patrol-wagons, 6 courts, and 3,200 men (each getting $800 to $1,200 a year). The headquarters is at 300 Mulberry Street, where the Rogues' Gallery is kept.

Distances.—Battery to City Hall, ¾ mile ; to Canal Street, 1¼ miles ; to 4th Street, 2 miles.   Above 3d Street the blocks between the streets bearing numbers are twenty to a mile, and the blocks between the avenues are seven to a mile.

RAILROAD DEPOTS.

THE following is a list of the principal railroads running into New York, the location of the depots, and how to reach the same from the *Grand Union Hotel,* Fourth Avenue and 42d Street (or *vice versa*). All the elevated railroads have stations at 42d Street. The directions are in Italic type.

Baltimore and Ohio Railroad. — Depot at Jersey City. Ferry from foot of Liberty Street. *Sixth-avenue Elevated Road to Cortlandt-street Station.*

Central Railroad of New Jersey. — Depot at Jersey City. Ferry from foot of Liberty Street. *Sixth-avenue Elevated Road to Cortlandt-street Station.*

Delaware, Lackawanna, and Western Railroad (Morris and Essex). — Depot at Hoboken. Ferry from foot of Barclay Street, or Christopher Street. *Ninth-avenue Elevated to Christopher-street Station,* or *Sixth-avenue Elevated to Park Place (for Barclay-street Ferry).*

Erie Railroad. — Depot at Jersey City. Ferry foot of Chambers Street, or West 23d Street. *Sixth-avenue Elevated to Chambers-street Station,* or *Third-avenue Elevated to 23d-street Station, and street-car across.*

Harlem Railroad. — See New York and Harlem.

Hudson-River Railroad. — See New-York Central and Hudson-River Railroad.

Long-Island Railroad. — Depot at Hunter's Point. Ferry from East 34th Street. *Street cars from door.*

Morris and Essex Railroad. — See Delaware, Lackawanna, and Western.

New-Jersey Central Railroad. — See Central Railroad of New Jersey.

New-Jersey Southern Railroad. — Depot at Sandy Hook. Steamer from foot of Rector Street. *Sixth-avenue Elevated to Rector Street.*

New-Jersey and New-York Railroad. — Depot at Jersey City. Ferry foot of Chambers Street and West 23d Street. *Sixth-avenue Elevated*

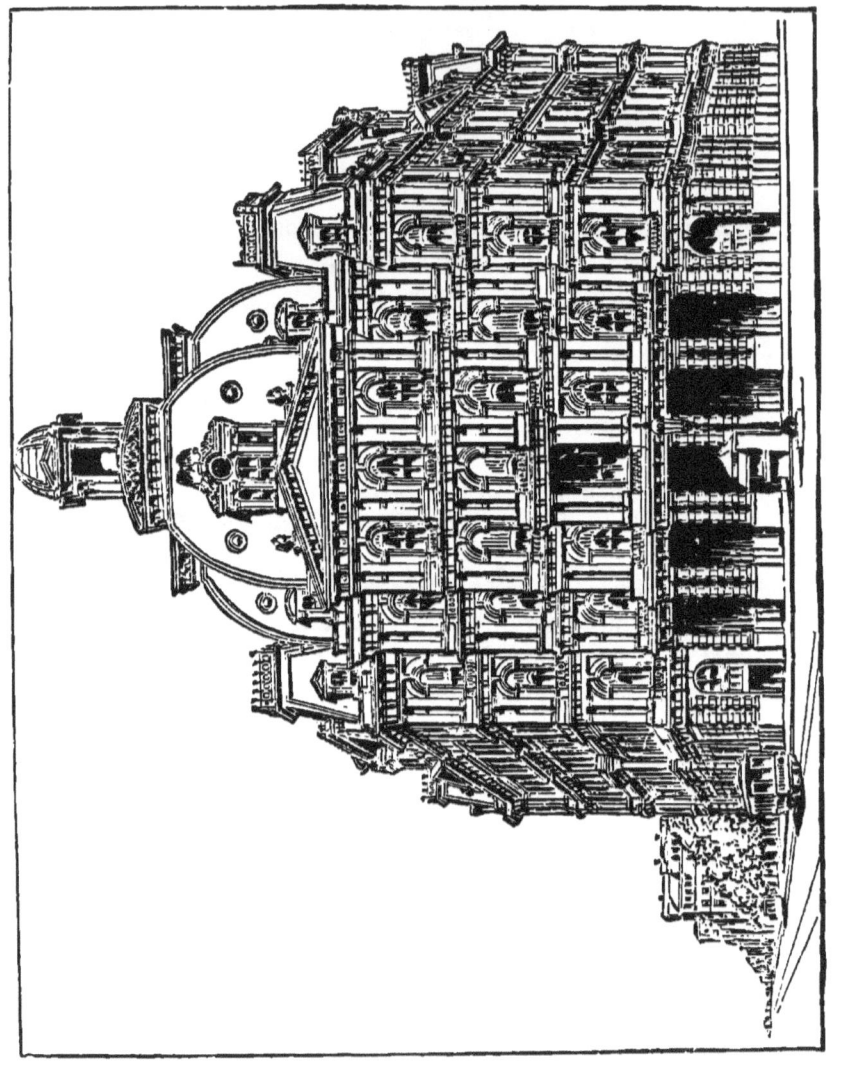

NEW-YORK POST-OFFICE.

to Chambers-street Station, or *Third-avenue Elevated to West-23d-street Station, and street-car across.*

New-York City and Northern Railroad. — Depot at 155th Street *Sixth-avenue Elevated Road.*

New-York Central and Hudson-River Railroad. — *Grand Central Depot.* (The *Grand Union Hotel* is just across the street.)

New-York and Harlem Railroad. — *Grand Central Depot.* (The *Grand Union Hotel* is just across the street.)

New-York, New-Haven, and Hartford Railroad. — *Grand Central Depot.* (The *Grand Union Hotel* is just across the street.)

New-York and New-England Railroad. — *Grand Central Depot.* (The *Grand Union Hotel* is just across the street.)

New-York, Ontario, and Western Railroad. — Depot at Weehawken Ferry from foot of West 42d Street. *42d-street Cross-town cars (white) pass the Grand Union Hotel, reaching the ferry in ten minutes.*

Pennsylvania Railroad. — Depot at Jersey City. Ferries at foot of Cortlandt Street and Desbrosses Street. *Sixth-avenue Elevated to Cortlandt Street,* or *Ninth-avenue to Desbrosses Street.*

Philadelphia and Reading Railroad. — Depot at foot of Liberty Street. *Sixth-avenue Elevated to Cortlandt Street.*

West-Shore Railroad. — Depots at Jersey City and Weehawken. Ferries from foot of Jay Street, and West 42d Street. *42d-street Cross-town cars (white) pass the Grand Union Hotel, reaching 42d street Ferry in ten minutes.*

THE OCEAN STEAMSHIP "MAJESTIC."

STEAMBOATS AND STEAMSHIPS.

Ocean Steamships.—All the principal transatlantic steamships sail from the port of New York. A visit to one of them will repay the stranger. Select a steamer of the American, Cunard, White Star, or French lines, and go down to the dock an hour or so before the sailing-time (see daily papers). The vessel will be crowded with passengers and their friends, the saloon gay with floral offerings, and every thing open to inspection. When the warning-bell rings, hurried farewells and parting injunctions and admonitions are given, and those who are to go on shore scurry down the gang-plank. Slowly the vessel backs out from the pier, and amid cheers and waving of handkerchiefs, and a chorus of good-bys, slowly turns her prow towards the many miles of trackless ocean which lie between her and her destination.

About this time the man who is always late comes rushing breathlessly down the pier, only to find that he is left again. It is of no avail for him frantically to wave his umbrella, and with shrill expostulation command the vessel to return. Those mighty engines will never cease to throb and pulse until the Old World is sighted.

The principal ocean lines sailing out of New York are,—

FOR EUROPE.

American Line.—New York to Southampton. Wednesdays. Pier 14, N. R., foot of Christopher Street. International Navigation Co., 6 Bowling Green.

Allen-State Line.—New York to Glasgow via Londonderry. Saturdays. Foot 21st Street, N. R. Austin Baldwin & Co., Agents, No. 53 Broadway.

Anchor Line.—New York to Glasgow. Saturdays. Pier 41 (new), N. R., foot of Leroy Street. Fares, first cabin, $50 to $60 ; second cabin, $30. Henderson Bros., Agents, No. 7 Bowling Green.

Anchor Line.—New York to Glasgow via Londonderry. Steamer " City of Rome." Every fourth Wednesday. Pier 41, N. R. Fares, first cabin, $60 to $100. Henderson Bros., Agents, No. 7 Bowling Green.

Cunard Line.—New York to Liverpool. Saturdays. Pier 40 (new), N. R., foot of Clarkson Street. Fares, first cabin, $60 to $125. Vernon H. Brown & Co., Agents, No. 4 Bowling Green.

French Line.—New York to Havre. Saturdays. Pier 42 (new), N. R., foot of Morton Street. Fares, first cabin, $80 to $100 ; second cabin, $60. A. Forget, General Agent, No. 3 Bowling Green.

Hamburg-American.—New York to Hamburg and Southampton. Thursdays and Saturdays. Pier foot of First Street, Hoboken. Fares, first cabin, single, $100 and up. Hamburg-American Packet Company, 37 Broadway.

Netherlands Line.—New York to Rotterdam or Amsterdam. Saturdays. Foot of Fifth Street, Hoboken. Fares, first cabin, $45 to $50 ; second cabin, $32.

North-German Lloyd.—New York to Bremen via Southampton. Wednesdays and Saturdays. Pier foot of Second Street, Hoboken. Fares, first cabin, $75 to $125 ; second cabin, $55. Oelrichs & Co., Agents, No. 2 Bowling Green.

Red-Star Line.—From New York to Antwerp and Paris. Saturdays. Pier foot of Sussex Street, Jersey City, adjoining Pennsylvania R. R. depot. Fares, first cabin, $45 and up ; second cabin, $35. Peter Wright & Sons, Agents, No. 5 Bowling Green.

White-Star Line.—New York to Liverpool. Wednesdays only.

Pier 45 (new), N. R., foot of West 10th Street. Fares, first cabin, $50 to $125 and up ; second cabin, $35. R. B. Ismay, Agent, No. 37 Broadway.

FOR BERMUDA AND WEST INDIES.

Quebec Steamship Company.—New York to Bermuda. Wednesdays. Pier 47 (new), N. R. Fares, first cabin, $30 ; excursion, $50 ; second cabin, $20 ; excursion, $33.50. A. E. Outerbridge & Co., Agents, No. 51 Broadway.

FOR CUBA AND MEXICO.

Compania Transatlantica Español.—New York to Havana. Every 10 days. Fulton Street, N. R. Fares, to Havana, first cabin, $50 ; to Vera Cruz, Mexico, first cabin, $85. J. M. Ceballos & Co., Agents, No. 80 Wall Street.

FOR CUBA, NASSAU, AND MEXICO.

New-York and Cuba Steamship Company. — New York to Havana. Wednesdays and Saturdays, 3 P.M. Pier 16, E. R. Fares, to Havana, $50 ; to Santiago and Cienfuegos, *via* South-side Line, $60 ; to Nassau, $40.

New-York and Cuba Steamship Company. — New York to Vera Cruz. Saturdays, 3 P.M. Pier 16, E. R. Fares, to Vera Cruz, $75 ; to City of Mexico, $80. James E. Ward & Co., Agents, No. 113 Wall Street.

FOR WEST INDIES AND SOUTH AND CENTRAL AMERICA.

Atlas Line. — New York to Kingston, Jamaica. Every 14 days. Pier 55, N. R. Fares, first cabin, $50 ; second cabin, $35. Pim, Forwood & Co., Agents, No. 22 State Street.

FOR ST. THOMAS AND SOUTH AMERICA.

United-States and Brazil Mail Steamship Company. — New York to St. Thomas and Rio de Janeiro. Monthly. Roberts' Stores, Brooklyn. Fares, first cabin to St. Thomas, $60; to Rio de Janeiro, $160. Paul F. Gerhard & Co., Agents, No. 84 Broad Street.

COASTWISE STEAMSHIPS.

The principal coastwise steamship lines sailing from the port of New York are, —

Cromwell Line. — New York to New Orleans, La. Wednesdays and Saturdays, 3 P.M. Pier 9, N. R. Fares, cabin, $35 ; Steerage. $20. S. II. Seaman, Agent, Pier 9, North River.

Mallory Line. — New York to Brunswick and Fernandina, Fla. Tuesdays and Fridays, 3 P.M. Pier 21, E. R. Fares, to Fernandina, first cabin, $22.50 ; to Jacksonville, $24.

Mallory Line. — New York to Galveston and Key West. Tuesdays, Thursdays, and Saturdays, 3 P.M. Pier 20, E. R. Fares to Galveston, Tex., $45 ; to Key West, Fla., $40. C. H. Mallory & Co., Agents, Pier 21, East River.

New York and Charleston Steamship Company. — New York to Charleston, S. C. Mondays, Wednesdays, and Fridays, 3 P.M. Pier 29, E. R. Fares, first cabin, $20 ; excursion, $32.

Ocean Steamship Company. — New York to Savannah. Mondays, Wednesdays, Fridays, and Saturdays, 3 P.M. New Pier 35, N. R., foot of Spring Street. Fares, first cabin, $20 ; excursion, $32. W. H. Rhett, Agent, No. 317 Broadway.

Old Dominion Line. — New York to Norfolk, Va. Tuesdays, Wednesdays, Thursdays, and Saturdays, 3 P.M. Pier 26 (new), N. R., foot of Beach Street. Fares, to Norfolk, Va., $8.00 ; excursion, $13.

Old Dominion Line. — New York to Richmond, Va. Wednesdays and Saturdays, 3 P.M. Pier 26, N. R. Fares, to Richmond, $9 ; excursion, $14. Old Dominion Company, No. 235 West Street.

River and Sound Steamboats. — Foreigners sailing into New-York Harbor for the first time are amazed at the grandeur of the River and Sound steamers. Nearly all are side-wheelers, usually painted white, and many are of great size and speed.

A LONG-ISLAND SOUND STEAMER.

The famous steamers " Massachusetts " and " Connecticut " of the Providence Line, from Pier 29, North River, run direct to Providence, connecting for Boston, Worcester, Nashua, Concord, White Mountains, Bar Harbor, and all points north and east. They are equipped with every luxury, and are veritable floating palaces.

For those who are not good sailors, and are troubled with seasick-ness, the "inside route" to Boston, *via* the Stonington Line, is always popular. It is entirely within the limits of Long Island Sound, and, except in cases of extreme weather, is usually a very quiet, easy, restful trip.

The principal lines, with their location, and the best way of reaching them from the Grand Union Hotel, are shown below. All Elevated Railroads have stations at 42d Street. N. R., = North River. E. R., = East River.

LONG-ISLAND SOUND STEAMERS.

Name of Line.	New York to —	Start from Foot of —	Elevated Station and Line Nearest.
Stonington Line.	Boston.	Spring St., N. R.	Desbrosses St., 9th Avenue.
Providence Line.	Boston.	Warren St., N. R.	Chambers St., 6th Avenue.
Norwich Line.	Boston.	Canal St., N. R.	Desbrosses St., 9th Avenue
Fall-River Line.	Boston.	Murray St., N. R.	Park Place, 6th Avenue.
Hartford Line.	Hartford.	Peck Slip, E. R.	Fulton St., 3d Avenue.
New-Haven Line.	New Haven.	Peck Slip, E. R.	Fulton St., 3d Avenue.
Bridgeport Line.	Bridgeport.	Peck Slip and Catherine St., E. R.	Fulton St., 3d Avenue, and Chatham Square, 3d Avenue.

HUDSON-RIVER STEAMERS.

Name of Line.	New York to —	Start from Foot of —	Elevated Station and Line Nearest.
People's Line.	Albany.	Canal St., N. R.	Desbrosses St., 9th Avenue.
Citizens' Line.	Albany and Troy.	Christopher St., N. R.	8th St., 6th Ave., and street-cars.
Day Line.	Albany and inter. points.	Vestry St., N. R.	Desbrosses St., 9th Avenue.

LOCAL MODES OF CONVEYANCE.

Elevated Railroads render getting about easy and rapid in New-York City, which being long and narrow, makes distances great. There are four of these roads; viz., the Second, Third, Sixth, and Ninth Avenue "*L*" lines. All of them extend the length of the city, and start from South Ferry, which is at the extreme lower end.

One branch of the Third-avenue line runs to and from the City Hall and Brooklyn Bridge to Chatham Square, where it joins the main line. Another branch runs through 42d Street to the *Grand Central Depot*, just across the street from which is the *Grand Union Hotel.* Another branch, on the Third and Second Avenue lines, runs from the 34th-street stations to the 34th-street Ferry. All the lines have stations at 42d Street, within easy distance of the Grand Central Depot and Grand Union Hotel. A good idea of the magnitude of the city may be obtained by taking the Third-avenue Elevated Road to South Ferry, changing there, and taking the Sixth-avenue line to 155th Street, and back to 42d Street, and walk or take horse-cars three blocks east to the hotel. The speed of the trains is about fifteen miles an hour.

For further particulars regarding Elevated Railroads, see end of book.

Horse-Cars.—There are over forty lines of horse or cable cars. Broadway and Third Avenue have been changed to cable. Space permits us to mention only a few of the principal ones :—

Broadway Line, from the Battery, up Broadway, to 45th Street, and thence up Seventh Avenue to Central Park (59th Street).

Madison-avenue Line, from Post-office to Fourth Avenue, up Fourth Avenue (passing Grand Union Hotel and Grand Central Depot), to Madison Avenue, to 138th Street.

Third-avenue Line, from Post-office to Third Avenue, and up Third Avenue (passing within one block of Grand Union Hotel and Grand Central Depot), to Harlem.

Sixth-avenue Line, from Broadway and Vesey Streets to Sixth Avenue, and up Sixth Avenue (passing within two blocks of Grand Union Hotel and Grand Central Depot), to Central Park (59th Street).

Belt Line, from Battery along the East-river front to 59th Street. across 59th Street, and down to Battery again on North-river front (west side). This line passes all ferries, steamboat and steamship docks.

Cross-town Lines cross the city from river to river, at Canal Street, Grand Street, Houston Street, 14th Street, 23d Street, 42d Street, 59th Street, and 125th Street, and also at Fulton Street.

Boulevard Line (green cars) passes through 42d Street, in front of Grand Union Hotel, up the Western Boulevard to Riverside Park and General Grant's tomb.

Fare. — The fare on all the lines is five cents.

Stages.—There is now but one line of stages (or omnibuses) in the city. The route is from the corner of South Fifth Avenue and Bleecker Street up Fifth Avenue to 89th Street. These stages, or coaches, are a great improvement over the "busses" used for so many years in New York. There are seats for twelve persons inside, and six on top. A ride the full length of this line, known as the "Fifth-avenue coaches," is strongly recommended, as it leads through a most superb part of the city. Ladies frequently ride on top, and there is no impropriety in so doing. The stages pass one block west of the Grand Union Hotel.

Fare.—The fare is five cents.

Cabs and Carriages. — Before hiring a cab or carriage, be sure to make an exact agreement with the driver as to the charge. Fares are high, but the driver will often try to get more than is legally due him ; and a wrangle is apt to ensue, unless a bargain is made beforehand.

Hansoms, or open London Cabs, have become very popular. It is easy to get in and out, and the passenger has an uninterrupted view. A pleasant way of seeing the city, is to hire one of these vehicles by the hour, and be driven through the principal streets. By applying at the hotel office, cabs or carriages with trustworthy drivers may be obtained at the regular rates, and no trouble will be had.

City Ordinances fix the legal rates for cabs and coaches, and make the following regulations : —

SECT. 89. — The price, or rates of fare, to be asked or demanded by the owners or drivers of hackney-coaches or cabs, shall be as fcl-lows : —

ONE-HORSE "CABS," OR "HANSOMS." 1. — For conveying one or more persons any distance, sums not exceeding the following amounts : fifty cents for the first mile or part thereof; and each additional half-mile or part thereof, twenty-five cents. By distance, for "stops" of over five minutes, and not exceeding fifteen minutes, twenty-five cents. For longer stops, the rate will be twenty-five cents for every fifteen minutes or fraction thereof, if more than five minutes. For a brief stop, not exceeding five minutes in a single trip, there will be no charge.

2. — For the use of a cab (or hansom) by the hour, with the privilege of going from place to place, and stopping as often and long as may be required, one dollar for the first hour or part thereof; and for each succeeding half-hour or part thereof, fifty cents.

TWO-HORSE "COACHES." 3. — For conveying one or more persons any distance, sums not exceeding the following amounts : one dollar for the first mile or part thereof; and each additional half-mile or part thereof, forty cents. By distance, for stops of over five minutes, and not exceeding fifteen minutes, thirty-eight cents. For longer stops, the rate will be thirty-eight cents for every fifteen minutes. For a brief stop, not exceeding five minutes in a single trip, there will be no charge.

4. — For the use of a coach by the hour, with privilege of going from place to place, and stopping as often and long as may be required, one dollar and fifty cents for the first hour or part thereof; and for each succeeding half-hour or part thereof, seventy-five cents.

5. — No cab or coach shall be driven the time-rate at a pace less than five miles an hour.

6. — From "line balls," one or two passengers, to any point south of 59th Street, two dollars; each additional passenger, fifty cents; north of 59th Street, each additional mile shall be charged for at a rate not to exceed fifty cents per mile.

7. — Every owner or driver of any hackney-coach or cab shall carry on his coach or cab one piece of baggage, not to exceed fifty pounds in weight, without extra charge; but for any additional baggage he may carry, he shall be entitled to extra compensation, at the rate of twenty-five cents per piece.

SECT. 100. — There shall be fixed in each hackney-coach or cab, in such a manner as can be conveniently read by any person riding in the same, a card containing the name of the owner of said carriage, the number of his license, and the whole of section 89 of this article, printed in plain, legible characters, under a penalty of revocation of license for violation thereof, said section to be provided by the License Bureau in pamphlet or card form, and to be furnished free to the owner of such hackney-coach or cab.

It shall be the duty of the driver of every such hackney-coach or cab, at the commencement of his employment, to present the passenger employing him with a printed card or slip containing, in case of cabs, subdivisions 1 and 2, and in case of coaches, subdivisions 3 and 4, of section 89 of this article.

SECT. 105. — Any person or persons who shall violate any or either of the provisions of sections 98 to 106, both inclusive, of this article shall be liable to a penalty of ten dollars.

PUBLIC BUILDINGS AND LOCALITIES.

WITH few exceptions, the public buildings of the city are not im posing or elegant. Most of them, built many years ago, suffer by contrast with the great commercial piles which have more recently been erected. The most important are named below.

Assay Office on Wall Street, just east of Nassau, is the oldest build ing on the street, having been built for the United-States Branch Bank, in 1823. Here gold and silver are brought in the crude state, and assayed, refined, and cast into bars, to be made into coin else where. As high as $100,000,000 in bullion is sometimes assayed here in a year. Here may be seen $50,000,000 or more, stacked up in shining gold bricks. Visitors are admitted between 10 A.M. and 2 P.M , and shown the various processes of assaying.

Castle Garden is at the extreme southern end of the city, in the Battery Park. It is now an aquarium. As it was the gateway of America to hundreds of thousands of immigrants, it has a deep in terest for all citizens. Of the 10,000,000 foreigners who have landed in our country in the past century, the majority have passed through this portal.

> Irish and Briton and Dutch though we be,
> We are each all Yank in our welcome by thee,
> Columbia.

Entering the enclosure, we see the fine old brown-stone ramparts of Castle Clinton, with its walled-up embrasures. The National Gov ernment built this fortress in 1807, and gave it to the city in 1823; and here were held the great popular receptions to Andrew Jackson (1832), President Tyler (1843), and Lafayette (1824). In later days it became a fashionable opera-house, where the grand voices of Sontag, Mario Parodi, and Jenny Lind were heard. In 1855 the immigrant depot was established here, for the reception of incomers from Europe.

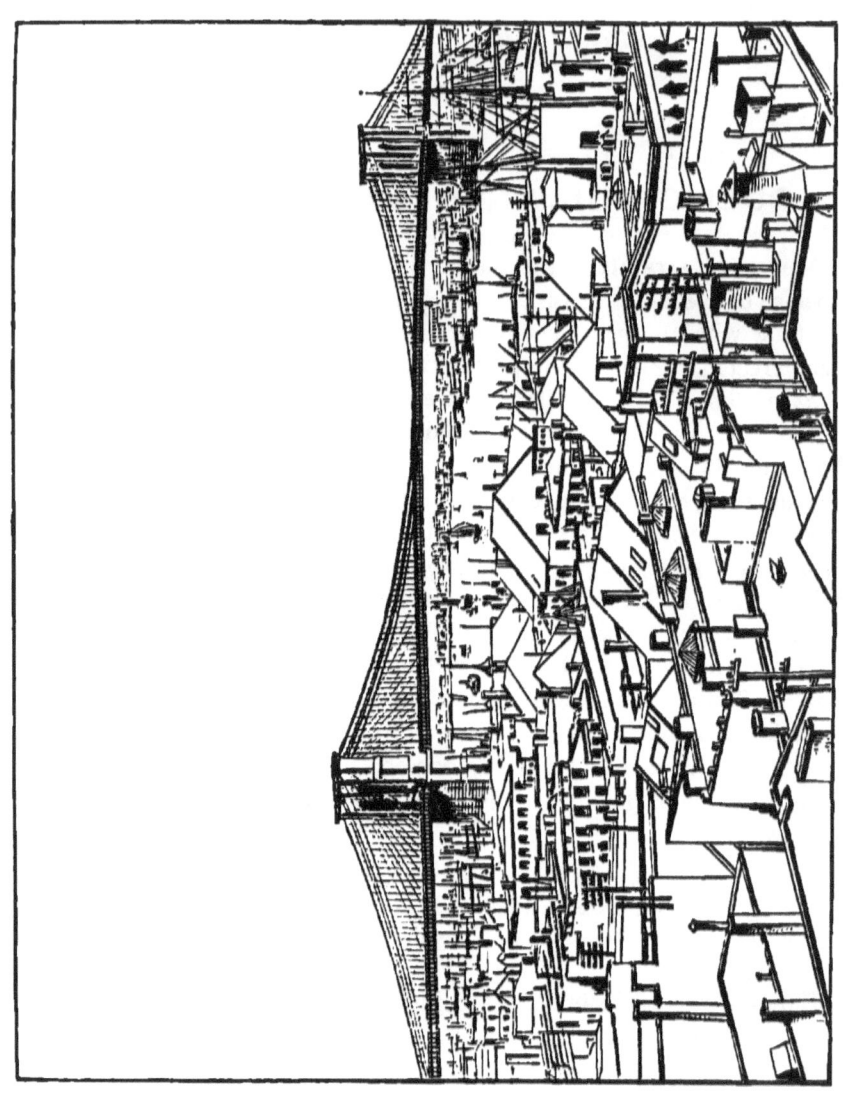

THE EAST-RIVER BRIDGE.

It is a most interesting sight when a steamship load of Italian or German immigrants debark with their strange baggage and appurtenances at the Barge Office.

City Hall, in the City-hall Park, was erected in 1803, in what was then the outskirts of the city. It is of white marble, built in the Italian style; the back being of brown-stone, as the authorities, eighty years ago, fancied that the town would never grow beyond it. The governor's room contains the desk on which Washington wrote his first message to Congress, the chair in which he was inaugurated, many historical portraits, and other objects of interest. A movement is now under way to build a new City Hall.

County Court House is on Chambers Street, near Broadway. It is a white marble building, in the Corinthian style, chiefly interesting as being the most costly building of its size ever erected. It was built in 1869-70, during the reign of William M. Tweed, the leader of the New-York "ring," when the city-debt increased nearly $50,000,000. Most of this amount was alleged to have been expended on this building. But the lion's share of it came back in the form of "rebates" and "commissions" to the guileless William and his associates. He afterwards died at Blackwell's Island. The Court House stands in the City-hall Park.

Custom House, on Wall Street, at the corner of William Street, is a large and sombre pile of Quincy granite. The portico is supported by 18 granite columns 38 feet high and 4½ feet in diameter, cut in one piece. The rotunda is a beautiful and lofty round hall, surrounded by pilasters of variegated marble. The Custom House cost $1,800,000.

East-River Bridge, or, more popularly, the "Brooklyn Bridge," spans the East River, and connects the cities of New York and Brooklyn. The length of the bridge is 5,989 feet, and it is 89 feet wide. It is suspended from four steel-wire cables, each 16 inches in diameter. In the centre is an elevated promenade, on each side of which is a railroad-track for passenger-cars propelled by a stationary engine. Outside of the railroad-track, on each side, are the roadways for vehicles. From the under side of the bridge, in the centre, to the water, is 135 feet. Ordinary vessels can easily pass beneath. Very large sailing-vessels have to lower their topmasts to go under. The fare for foot-passengers has been abolished and the promenade is now free. The single fare on the cars is 3 cents, or ten tickets for 25 cents. Several "cranks" have leaped off the bridge into the river, bent on suicide, or achieving notoriety. Up to the present time, only one has been killed, the others having unfortunately survived. The total cost of the bridge was $15,000,000. It is a notable experience .o walk across the bridge by the elevated footway, on a calm and pleasant day, and get the noble panoramic views of the two great cities, and the thronged river and harbor. This wonderful pontifical work, the greatest in the world, was built between 1870 and 1883. 15,000,000 persons cross the bridge annually. The piers reach a height of 272 feet above high tide, and rest on caissons of yellow pine, iron, and concrete, sunk in the bed of the river. There is wire enough used in the cables to stretch nearly ⅞ of the way around the world. To go to the Bridge, take the City-hall train on the Third-avenue Elevated Road.

High Bridge, by which the Croton Aqueduct is carried across the Harlem River, at 175th Street, in cast-iron pipes 7½ × 8½ feet in size, is a very picturesque and noble stone structure of 13 arches, over 100 feet above the river, and 1,400 feet long. Half-a-mile above is the new and magnificent *Washington Bridge*.

Jefferson-Market Court and Prison is a picturesquely irregular pile at the corner of Sixth Avenue and 10th Street, of brick and sandstone, in Lombardo-Gothic architecture. At one corner is a fine round tower of graceful and effective proportions.

Ludlow-Street Jail, near Essex Market and Grand Street, is a massive brick structure for debtors, United-States prisoners, and derelict militia-men. Among its guests have been Tweed, Connolly, Fish, Ward, and other notorious politicians and financiers of New York.

Navy Yard.—Wallabout Bay, Brooklyn. (Cross Fulton Ferry, and take horse-cars.) The principal naval station of the country, and of melancholy interest as illustrating the decay of the American navy.

The yard contains an enormous stone dry-dock (built at a cost of $2,000,000), a museum, a library, and a number of venerable vessels-of-war of an obsolete and now wholly useless type. At the approach of a Presidential election, the yard presents a scene of great activity; many hundreds of voters being engaged in taking down piles of material, and then piling them up again, at liberal wages. The great Marine Barracks and Marine Hospital are worthy of notice; and also the parks of artillery, including many trophy-guns, captured in battle, from Mexican and other foes. In the British prison-ships moored in Wallabout Bay, 11,500 Americans died during the Revolutionary war. They are buried near by.

Post-Office, at the junction of Broadway and Park Row, is an immense triangular building of Dix-Island (Maine) granite, which cost nearly $7,000,000, and was finished in 1875. Over 600,000,000 letters, newspapers, etc., are handled here annually. The office yields a profit, annually, of nearly $3,000,000, and is the largest in the United States.

Register's Office, just east of the City Hall, was the British provost prison during the Revolutionary war, where many patriots were confined.

State Arsenal is a gray-stone building with turrets, at Seventh Avenue and 35th Street, the headquarters of the State Ordnance and Quartermaster's Departments, and a militia brigade.

Sub-Treasury, at the corner of Wall and Nassau Streets, a noble Doric building of white granite, covers the spot where Washington was inaugurated President. Here the City Hall was built, in 1700, with the cage, whipping-post, pillory, and stocks in front. The first United-States Congress under the Constitution met here, when it was named FEDERAL HALL; and for some years it was the State Capitol. The present building was erected and long used for the Custom House. On its roof four pieces of light artillery are kept, and rifle-men guard the premises at night. It contains vaults for the storage of gold and silver coin, notes, etc. On the granite steps in front stands a colossal bronze statue of Washington, by J. Q. A. Ward. The pedestal contains the stone on which Washington stood when he took the oath of office in April, 1789. There is an impressive classic portico facing Broad Street.

Tombs, the popular name given to the city prison, occupies the block bounded by Centre, Elm, Leonard, and Franklin Streets, and is a large and gloomy granite building in the pure Egyptian style.   Visitors are admitted on application at the office of the Commissioners of Charity and Corrections, corner of Third Avenue and 11th Street.   Sometimes more than five hundred prisoners are incarcerated within these frowning walls,—murderers, incendiaries, burglars, thieves, and all their horrid crew.   The murderers' cells are of especial strength. The building dates from 1838, and holds prisoners awaiting trial, and convicts waiting to be executed, or sent to the State prison.   The Tombs Police Court is held here.   On this site in ancient times rippled the blue waters of a pretty lake, around which the Indians built their wigwams.   The Dutch found their mounds of shells here, and named the place Kalk-Hook, or Lime-shell Point, which degenerated into "The Collect."   It was near the pond on this site, in the year 1626, that three of Minuit's farm-hands murdered a Weckquaesgeek Indian, who was bringing his furs down to sell.   His young nephew escaped, and afterwards led the Indians in disastrous and vengeful forays on the colony.   Knox's American infantry marched in to the Fresh-water Pond, and sat here in the long grass, while the British army was embarking from New York, in 1783.   Here, in 1796, occurred the first trial of a steamboat with a screw-propeller, John Fitch's invention.

PARKS AND SQUARES.

Central Park, the most beautiful and popular public domain in America, only thirty years ago was a dreary region of swamps, thickets, and ledges, disfigured with heaps of cinders and rubbish, and dotted with the squalid shanties of degraded squatters. Since then a paradise has been created here, by an outlay of upwards of $15,000,000. Winding lakelets and velvet lawns have succeeded the gloomy swamps, splendid driveways curve around the picturesque rocky knolls, footpaths meander through the groves and thickets, and fine architecture and monuments of art are seen on every side. The Park extends from 59th Street to 110th Street (over 2½ miles), and from Fifth Avenue to Eighth Avenue (over ½ mile), covering 862 acres, of which 185 are in lakes and reservoirs, and 400 in forests, wherein over half a million trees and shrubs have been planted. There are 9 miles of roads, 5¼ of bridle-paths, and 28¼ of walks. The landscape architects of the Park were Frederick Law Olmsted and Calvert Vaux. Upwards of 12,000,000 people visit the Park every year, half of them on foot.

The best way to get a general idea of this great pleasure-ground is to take one of the large public park-carriages, at the entrances on Fifth Avenue and Eighth Avenue. The fare to Mount St. Vincent, in the northern part, and return, is twenty-five cents.

In the south-west part of the Park is the Ball-Ground, — a ten-acre lawn, where the boys may play cricket, base-ball, or tennis; and adjoining it on the north-east is the *Carrousel,* for young children, with swings and other means of amusement. Close by is the Dairy, affording milk and light food for the little ones. Beyond is the Green, or Common, a lawn of 16 acres, made picturesque by grazing sheep, and thrown open to the people on Saturday. In the south-east part is the Menagerie, around the old castellated Arsenal building, and with many cages for animals, birds, a house full of monkeys of various kinds, bear-pits with amiable appearing ursine dwellers, and many other wild creatures,

THE MALL—CENTRAL PARK.

whose movements are watched by thousands of visitors daily. In winter, when several circuses board their animals here, the resident population is augmented by sundry lions, tigers, bisons, leopards, camels, hippopotami, and other rare and interesting sojourners.

The Mall is the chief promenade, nearly a quarter of a mile long, and 208 feet wide, bordered by double rows of American elms, with the Green on one side, and a bold, rocky ridge on the other. Here are the statues of Scott, Shakspeare, Burns, Fitz-Greene Halleck, the colossal Beethoven bust, and other artistic memorials. Beyond the Music Pavilion, where band-music is given on pleasant Saturday afternoons, is the Terrace, a sumptuous pile of light Albert-freestone masonry, with arcades and corridors, and rich carvings of birds and animals. Below is the Lower Terrace, an ornamental esplanade, in which stands the famous Bethesda Fountain, designed by Emma Stebbins, and made at Munich, and representing a lily-bearing angel, descending, and blessing the outflowing waters. Close by extends the Lake, 20 acres of winding water, devoted to public pleasure-boats in summer, and skating in winter. This part of the Park is reached direct from the 72d-street Station of the Third-avenue or Sixth-avenue Elevated railroads. Beyond the Lake is the Ramble, a delightful labyrinth of footpaths amid thickets, rocks, and streams. Farther on rises the Belvedere, a tall Norman tower of stone, overlooking the Park and the suburbs of New York, the Palisades, Long Island, Orange Mountain, and Westchester County. Next come the great reservoirs of Croton water, vast granite-walled structures containing 1,200,000 gallons of water. The American Museum of Natural History is on the left, on Manhattan Square, a kind of annex to the Park, between 77th and 81st Streets and Eighth and Ninth Avenues. The Metropolitan Museum of Art (see chapter on ART GALLERIES) is on the right, near 82d Street.

Beyond the reservoirs extend the North Park, with the carriage-concourse on Great Hill; the North Meadow, of 19 acres; Harlem Meer, covering 12½ acres, and overlooked by ancient fortifications; and the deep ravine of M'Gowan's Pass, from which Leslie's British light-infantry drove the Continental troops, in September, 1776. Just beyond, on the plains of Harlem, the Maryland line came to the rescue of the retreating Virginians and Connecticut Rangers, and drove the British back, with heavy losses.

Riverside Park occupies the high bank of the Hudson, from 72d to 130th Street, 3 miles long, and averaging 500 feet wide, with 178 acres of land, much of which has been improved by landscape gardening. A magnificent driveway, cut into four broad sections by curving ribbons of lawns and trees, sweeps over the hills and along the edge of the bluff, affording very charming views of the Hudson River, Weehawken, Guttenberg, Edgewater, the Palisades, and upper Manhattan. On a noble elevation near the north end of the Park is the brick tomb in which Gen. Grant's body was temporarily laid, with imposing cere-monies, Aug. 8, 1885. You can look through the latticed door, and see the flower-laden receptacle in which the remains of the great hero are placed. Near the tomb is the old Claremont mansion. People who want to see Grant's tomb only, can go up on the Sixth-avenue Elevated to 125th Street, and thence go west on 122d Street and Riverside Avenue. Those who wish to ride through the whole park, with its lovely views of Weehawken and beyond, can take park-coaches (twenty-five cents) from the Elevated station at Ninth Avenue and 72d Street. Around this wonderfully beautiful strip of park it is said will be the patrician residence-quarter of the New York of the twentieth century.

Among the other public grounds of the great metropolis, we may mention a few of the most important.

Battery (the) is the oldest park in the city. It covers 21 acres at the seaward end of the island, with trees, lawns, and walks, and a fine promenade around the sea-wall. Here stood the Battery erected by the Dutch founders of the city; and in later days, the aristocratic houses of the city fronted on its lawns. Sir Guy Carleton's British army embarked here on Nov. 25, 1783, a date still celebrated as EVACUATION DAY. On one side is Castle Garden, and on another the United-States Revenue Barge-Office. Here the Elevated Railways terminate. There are beautiful harbor-views from the sea-wall. In

July, 1776, the British frigates " Rose " and " Phœnix," with their decks protected by sand-bags, ran by the roaring Battery and up the Hudson, firing broadsides on to the town.

Bowling Green, at the foot of Broadway, is a little oval park, with a weary fountain in its centre, and surrounded by ocean-steamship offices, foreign consulates, etc., and the great Produce Exchange, Washington Building, and Standard Oil Company's Building. On the site of the Washington Building (Cyrus W. Field's), in 1760 Archibald Kennedy, the collector of the port, built a large house, which afterwards became the headquarters of Lords Cornwallis and Howe, and Sir Henry Clinton and George Washington. Here also Talleyrand made his home. No. 3 Broadway was Benedict Arnold's dwelling. At No. 11, on the site of Burgomaster Kruger's Dutch tavern, was Gen. Gage's headquarters, in the old King's-Arms Inn. The Green was a treaty-ground with the Indians, the parade for the Dutch train-bands, and a cattle-market. In 1732 it was enclosed "for the beauty and ornament of said street, as well as for the delight of the inhabitants of this city." The present iron fence dates from 1770, and was formerly capped with round balls, which were knocked off, and used as cannon-balls by our artillery in the Revolution. In 1626, soon after Peter Minuit, first governor of New Netherlands, had arrived in the ship "Sea Mew," and bought the island of Manhattan from the natives for $26, he built here Fort Amsterdam, a blockhouse surrounded by a cedar palisade. Seven years later it was enlarged by Wouter Van Twiller, and garrisoned by one hundred and four rotund Dutch soldiers. This site is now occupied by the block of six old-fashioned brick buildings south of the square. On the site of the Produce Exchange, in 1633, Wouter Van Twiller built the first church on Manhattan, and a house for his good Dutch dominie. On the site of the fort, a stately Ionic-porticoed mansion was built in 1790, for the Presidential palace, and became the official residence of Gov. George Clinton and John Jay. In 1815 it was replaced by the Bowling-Green Block. No. 39 Broadway was the site of the first European dwelling on Manhattan, built in 1612 by Hendrick Christiaensen, the agent of the Dutch fur-trading company, who raised here

HIGH BRIDGE (page 26).

four small houses and a redoubt, the foundation of the present great city. Christiaensen was killed by an Indian afterwards, this being the first murder on record in the province. In July, 1776, to celebrate the Declaration of Independence, the people came down here in vast crowds, and knocked over the equestrian statue of George III., which was melted into bullets to assimilate with the brains of the adversary. The great fire of 1776, which destroyed the greater part of New York, began near Whitehall Slip, and swept over the city on a strong south wind, while the angry British garrison bayonetted many of the citizens, and threw others, screeching, into the sea of flame. Chancellor Livingston lived on lower Broadway, in a house hung with Gobelin tapestry and rare paintings, with a $30,000 dinner-service of solid silver, and a rural palace at Clermont, up the Hudson.

Hanover Square is at the corner of Pearl and William Streets, with an elevated-railroad station, and is now the centre of the wholesale cotton-trade in America. On one side is the old Cotton Exchange, and on another side is the imposing new Cotton Exchange. Hereabouts, a century or more ago, were the mansions of the Beekmans, Hamersleys, Gouverneurs, Hoffmans, and Van Hornes. And here Admiral Digby entertained Prince William Henry, afterwards William IV. of England. About Hanover Square, in 1800, dwelt a community of French *émigrés*, — De Neuville, La Rue, De Rivière, and others; and the famous Gen. Moreau, sometime commander of the Army of the Rhine and Moselle, banished by Napoleon, who, after dwelling here for seven years, joined the Allied armies in Europe, and was killed at the battle of Dresden by a cannon-shot, aimed by Napoleon himself.

Jeannette Park, near Hanover Square, has recently been made by filling up the ancient Coenties Slip.

Chatham Square, at the intersection of Chatham Street, East Broadway, and the Bowery, is the concurrent point of several elevated and horse railways, and one of the most crowded and busy localities in this roaring metropolis. A hundred years ago, the marshes hereabouts were so pestilent, that their owner, Rutgers, declared "the inhabitants lose one-third of their time by sickness."

City-Hall Park covers about 8 acres, partly bounded by resounding Broadway, and the newspaper-abounding Park Row, and contains the City Hall, Court House, and other well-worn public buildings. Here, also, fronts the United-States Post-Office, a mountain of granite. Before the Revolution, it was an open field, in the country, where the people used to assemble for great popular demonstrations.

Franklin Square, five minutes' walk east of City-hall Square, down Frankfort Street, used to be a hillock between the Swamp and the East River. It has the Brooklyn Bridge on one side, and the great Harper's publishing-house on another, and is roofed over by the Elevated-railway trestles. At Cherry Street and Franklin Square, Walter Franklin, the great Russian merchant, built a palace, which became the Presidential mansion, where Washington held his court, and gave his brilliant receptions.

Printing-House Square, just east of the City Hall, contains most of the great newspaper offices, the " Tribune," " Times," " Sun," " World," " News," " Journal," " Mail and Express," and many others, with scores of famous and widely influential weekly papers. Here the great presses thunder on, night and day, printing their varied editions ; reporters flit to and fro with " copy ; " and the wonderful New-York newspapers are made up, with all their teeming freightage of battle and murder and sudden death, lectures, political leaders, and the annals of the passing day. The most picturesque and brilliant of these great metropolitan journals is " The World," with its army of able writers, and its colossal editions, consuming this year over a million dollars' worth of paper alone.

Union Square is a park of 3½ acres, with fountains, trees, statues of Lincoln and Washington, electric lights, and other bravery, between 14th and 17th Streets and Broadway and Fourth Avenue. All around are hotels, restaurants, theatres, shops, and offices, the centre of an ever busy and picturesque life. Its northern part is an open *plaza* for parades, with a platform for speakers or reviewing-officers.

Washington Square covers 9 acres, at the lower end of Fifth Avenue, between Waverley Place and 4th Street. (See page 96.)

Madison Square covers 6 acres, between Broadway and Madison

Avenue and 23d and 26th Streets, and has lawns and trees, statues of Seward and Farragut, and a tall electric-light tower. Around it are stores, huge hotels, restaurants, and famous club-houses. It is the central point of the life and splendor of upper New York.

Gramercy Park, 1½ acre, between 20th and 21st Streets and Third and Fourth Avenues, a part of the old Gramercy farm, is a private *plaisaunce,* around which are the homes of many old families, — John Bigelow (No. 21), Cyrus W. Field (123 East 21st Street), David Dudley Field (64 Park Avenue), Max Strakosch, and others. Here was the palatial home of the late Samuel J. Tilden (No. 15).

Stuyvesant Square, on a part of the old Stuyvesant farm, covers 4 acres, between East 15th and 17th Streets, with the tall twin spires of St. George's overlooking it. In this vicinity dwelt Hamilton Fish (ex-Secretary of State), Sidney Webster, Jackson S. Schultz, Russell Sturgis, Richard H. Stoddard (the poet), William H. Schieffelin, the Rutherfords, the Stuyvesants, and other well-known persons. The square has rich and luxuriant foliage and lawns, the local paradise for the dwellers in the adjacent crowded tenement region of the east side.

Tompkins Square covers ten acres of lawns and greenery, between East 7th and 10th Streets and Avenues A and B, surrounded by one of the most overcrowded tenement regions of the East side.

Bryant Park is a pleasant open space, between 40th Street and 42d Street, and Sixth Avenue and the Reservoir, which received its present name in 1884, in honor of William Cullen Bryant. On this site the world-renowned Crystal Palace stood in those far-away days before the war. It is now a favorite resort of West-side children.

Morningside Park, a long-drawn and nearly unimproved public ground of 47 acres, extends from 110th Street to 123d Street, near Tenth Avenue, and has a costly and far-viewing driveway. It lies on the east, or morning, side of the ridge which separates Harlem plains from the Riverside Park and Hudson River.

Mount Morris Square surrounds a bold, rocky hill, by which even the lordly Fifth Avenue is stopped, in the environs of Harlem. It abounds in maples, tulip-trees, oaks, etc.; and from the *plaza* near the fire-alarm tower, on the crest of the hill, a broad view is enjoyed.

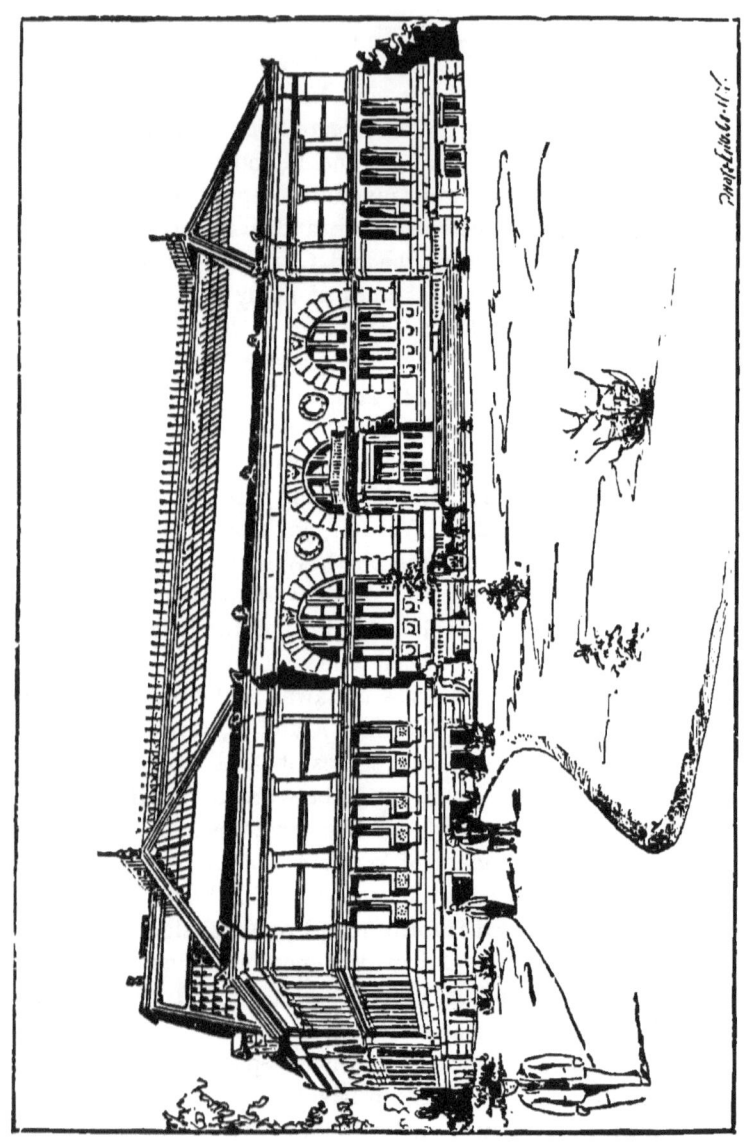

THE METROPOLITAN MUSEUM OF ART.

ART-GALLERIES.

Metropolitan Museum of Art, in Central Park, near Fifth Avenue and 83d Street. 25 cts. entrance on Mond. and Tues., but free other days, including Sundays. A great collection of Dutch and Flemish pictures, and other European works of art. It may be reached by Elevated Railway from the Grand Union Hotel, to the station at Third Avenue and 84th Street, or by the Madison-avenue horse-cars. The first movement towards founding the Museum was made in 1869, and for some years its collections were kept in rented buildings down town (14th Street). The present fireproof brick and granite modern-Gothic building was dedicated in 1880, by the President of the United States. It is 233 by 224 feet in area ; and new structures are being built in connection, so that in time it will be one of the greatest art-museums in the world. Space fails to tell of the beauties of these varied and extensive collections, numbering many thousands of pieces. Pamphlet catalogues are for sale at the door, for ten cents each, one for the Loan Collection of Paintings, one for the Old Masters, one for the Cesnola Collection, etc. The pleasure of a visit will be much heightened by their aid. A long rainy day can be profitably and charmingly spent at the Museum. In the West-entrance Hall are many fine pieces of statuary, Beer's Medallion of Michael Angelo, the Apollo Belvedere, Hiram Powers's "California," "George Washington," "Alexander I. of Russia," Roncanelli's "Rose of Sharon," Albano's "Thief" from Dante's "Inferno," Mozier's "Rizpah," Fischer's "Goethe," McDonald's "Gen. Hancock," Schwanthaler's "Dancing Girl," Marochetti's "Washington," Houdon's "Franklin," Conelly's "Thetis;" and many fine works by Barye, Barbedienne, Thorwaldsen, Reinhart, Canova, Launt Thompson, *et als.,* loaned by their owners. Here also is the Poe Memorial, presented to the Museum by the actors of New York. On the south-west stairway is a collection of 43 water-colors by William T. Richards, of New-England coast and White-Mountain scenes.   The great hall contains many pieces of the famous Cesnola collection, from Cyprus, and various other interesting collections of rare objects of art.   In the galleries are the collections of gold jewellery and Greek and Phœnician glass from the Cesnola treasure-trove ; and also the Japanese, Egyptian, and Oriental porcelain and antiquities. Among the art-treasures in the western galleries are many of Kensett's exquisite landscapes, Gifford's and Durand's masterpieces, Frère's Oriental scenes, Couture's " Decadence of Rome," Maignan's " Outrage at Anagni," Madrazo's portrait of Robert L. Stuart, Bonnat's portrait of John Tayler Johnston, Meyer von Bremen's *genre* pictures, Granet's " Benedictines," Hellquist's great Swedish historical scene, Wylie's " Death of a Vendéan Chief," William M. Hunt's " Boy and Butterfly," Marr's " Mystery of Life ; " landscapes by Cropsey, Inness, and Breton ; Boughton's famous " Judgment of Wouter Van Twiller," Schreyer's Arab scenes, and many other noble and almost priceless works of art.   The East Gallery is devoted to pictures by the old masters, — Baroccio, Albani, Titian, Correggio, Tiarini, Caravaggio, Tintoretto, Tiepolo, Sassoferrato, Bordone, Andrea del Sarto, Ghirlandajo, Rembrandt, Rubens, Jordaens, Hals, Van Dyck, Cuyp, Wouverman, Ostade, Teniers, Terburg, Breughel, Ruysdael, Steen, Velazquez, Murillo, Copley, Stuart, Trumbull, Jarvis, Etty, Lely, Poussin.   Rubens's " Return of the Holy Family from Egypt " was painted on wood for the Jesuit Church at Antwerp, and after the suppression of the Jesuits, in 1777, passed to London.   His " Lions Chasing Deer " came from Cardinal Fieschi's collection.   Many other pictures in this remarkable collection have romantic histories, extending over centuries.   Rosa Bonheur's " Horse Fair," purchased at the Stewart sale for fifty-nine thousand dollars, has just been presented by Cornelius Vanderbilt; and the magnificent collection of paintings bequeathed to the museum by the late Catherine Wolf has recently been added, and is in an annex building erected for its reception.

Lenox Library's Picture-Gallery (Fifth Avenue and 71st Street) has about 150 fine paintings, including Munkacsy's " Blind Milton dictating Paradise Lost to his Daughters," Turner's " A Scene on the French Coast " and " Fingal's Cave " Horace Vernet's " Siege of Sara

gossa," Gainsborough's " A Romantic Woody Landscape," Andrea del
Sarto's " Tobit and the Angel," Delaroche's " The Field of Battle,"
Church's "Cotopaxi," Thomas Cole's "Expulsion from Paradise,"
Bierstadt's " Yo Semite," Sir Joshua Reynolds's portraits of Edmund
Burke, Kitty Fisher, and Mrs. Billington ; portraits by Leslie, Stuart,
Newton, Trumbull, Inman, Peale, Copley, Daniel Huntington, S. F.
B. Morse, Healy, Pine, and others ; and original paintings of dogs by
Landseer ; sheep by Verboeckhoven ; landscapes by Mulready, Con-
stable, Kensett, George L. Brown, Durand, and Ruysdael ; and classi-
cal subjects by Sir David Wilkie.   The statuary includes Crawford's
"Sleeping Shepherd Boy" and "Children in the Wood," Rauch's
"Victory," Powers's "La Penserosa," Ball's "Abraham Lincoln," Sir
John Steele's "Sir Walter Scott," Trentanove's "Napoleon," etc.

Society of American Artists, 152 West 57th Street, organized in 1877,
gives annual spring exhibitions.

American Water-Color Society rooms are at 51 West 10th Street.

Society of Decorative Art has classes, library, and sales-rooms at 28
East 21st Street.   Its members are women.

National Academy of Design, at 23d Street and Fourth Avenue, is a
study in dark-blue stone and white Westchester marble of thirteenth-
century Gothic architecture, forming a peculiarly lovely and artistic
façade.   The great exhibition galleries, on the third floor, are reached
by an imposing oak and marble staircase ; and here are held exhibitions
of paintings for two months every spring.   The carved capitals of the
columns were careful studies from leaves and flowers.   The anvil-
wrought iron-work is remarkable for its finish and strength.   Notice
the beautiful Gothic entrance and drinking-fountain.   Daniel Huntington is president of the National Academy, and T. Addison Richards
is secretary.   The National Academicians (N. A.) are chosen annually
from the Associates (A. N. A.).   *From the Grand Union Hotel, take
Madison-avenue horse-cars to 23d Street.*

American Art-Gallery is in Kurtz's Building, at 6 East 23d Street.
Fourth-avenue horse-cars to 23d Street.

New-York Historical Society, 170 Second Avenue, corner of East
11th Street, has in its gallery 1,000 pictures, many of them by the old

GENERAL GRANT'S TOMB (page 32).

masters, and 100 pieces of statuary. This magnificent collection, the finest in America, is unfortunately sealed against the
public, except such as secure an introduction from members of
the Society.

Sarony's, the famous photograph gallery at 37 Union Square, has
a rare and interesting collection of weapons, armor, pictures, statuary,
and other *bric-à-brac*, quite worthy of a visit.

Art-rooms and Art-stores are numerous ; and many should be vis-
ited, to see the fine modern paintings, etchings, bronzes, etc. Knoed-
ler's (formerly Goupil's), 355 Fifth Avenue. Avery's, 368 Fifth
Avenue. Schaus's, Fifth Avenue, near 26th Street. Kohn's, 166
Fifth Avenue. Cottier's, 144 Fifth Avenue. Sarony's, 37 Union
Square. Keppel's (rare engravings and etchings), 23 E. 16th Street.
Interesting antiques may be seen at Feuardent's, 30 Lafayette Place,
and Sypher's, 246 Fifth Avenue.

Private Galleries of the Vanderbilts, Belmont, Hilton, and Mar-
quand are very rich in fine paintings, but may not be visited by
strangers unaccredited.

Hoffman House, in its bar-room, parlors, and rotunda, has several of
the finest and costliest art-works in America, including pictures by
Correggio and Bouguereau, a large Gobelin tapestry, and other
pieces. It is often visited by ladies.

Studios of artists occupy the Sherwood Building, Sixth Avenue and
57th Street; the Studio Building, 51 West 10th Street, between Fifth
and Sixth Avenues ; and the Fourth-avenue Studio Building, Fourth
Avenue, corner of 25th Street. There are also many studios in the
Young Men's Christian Association Building, Fourth Avenue and 23d
Street; the Studio Building, Broadway and 28th Street; the Rembrandt, West 57th Street, near Seventh Avenue; the Holbein, 139-145
West 55th Street; and No. 108 West 55th Street. In the Sherwood
are the studios of Bolton Jones, Deluce, Fredericks, Beckwith, Gran-
ville Perkins, Curran, etc. In the Rembrandt are the Giffords and
Sartain, and Junius Henri Browne, the literarian. Many of the artists
have regular reception-days, when visitors are made welcome.

Art-School of Cooper Union, Third Avenue and 7th Street.

Art-School of National Academy of Design, Fourth Ave. and 23d St.

Art-Students' League, 143 East 23d Street, under C. R. Lamb's presidency.

School of Industrial Art, for women, 251 West 23d St.

Women's Institute of Technical Design, 124 Fifth Avenue.

Metropolitan Museum of Art Schools, Central Park, opp. E. 82d St.

THE MILITIA.

THE disciplined militia of the city numbers 5,250 men, in eight regiments of infantry, two batteries of artillery, one troop and signal corps. They are equipped by the State with arms and other munitions, and partly with uniforms ; and the term of enlistment is five years. In winter, there are continual company-drills ; and in summer, several days of camp-duty under canvas, at the State camp-ground near Peekskill. Besides adding an element of military splendor to the sober burgher life of the city, they are of utmost service in preserving the public peace on the rare occasions when riots or other public disturbances are under way, and the police need behind them the moral effect of long lines of bayonets and loaded rifles. They have swept the tumultuous streets with deadly volleys more than once, and were equally efficient in line of battle before Gen. Lee's ragged but heroic Southern infantry.

Seventh Regiment Armory covers the entire block bounded by 66th and 67th Streets, and Fourth and Lexington Avenues. The main drill-room is 200 by 300 feet. The company and veterans' rooms are very elegantly furnished ; and there are library, reception, and memorial rooms of much beauty. The building is open to visitors. Two companies drill each evening. It was built in 1879, at a cost of $300,000. (Col. Daniel A. Appleton.)

Eighth Regiment Armory is at Park Avenue and 94th Street.

Ninth Regiment Armory is at 221 West 26th Street. (Col. William Seward.)

Twelfth Regiment Armory is on Ninth Avenue, from 61st Street to 62d Street, ponderous, castellated, with heavily grated windows, loopholed towers, and a high castle-keep. Within, besides many company-rooms, etc., is an enormous drill-hall, handsomely equipped.

Twenty-second Regiment Armory is a spacious and attractive structure on Boulevard and 67th Street.

Sixty-ninth Regiment Armory is over Tompkins Market, on Third Avenue, between 6th and 7th Streets. This is the famous Irish regiment that did such noble service under Col. Corcoran in the Secession war.

Seventy-first Regiment Armory is at Park Avenue and 34th Street. One of its quaintest trophies is a cannon, "captured from the Bowery Boys" in the famous Dead-Rabbit war, in 1857. This was one of the bravest commands in the Battle of Bull Run.

THE STATUE OF LIBERTY.

STATUES.

THE objects which a stranger usually wants to see in New York first are the Statue of Liberty and the East-river Bridge, the greatest works of their kind in the world.

Statue of "Liberty Enlightening the World" stands on Bedloe's Island, in the harbor. It is a majestic female figure made of copper, 151 feet 1 inch high, standing on a pedestal 154 feet 10 inches high. It was modelled by Bartholdi, a French sculptor, and was presented by the French people to the people of the United States. In the upraised right hand is a torch, lighted by electricity; and in the left hand is the Constitution. The copper is about ⅛ of an inch thick. The forefinger is 8 feet long and 5 feet in circumference. The finger-nail is 14 inches long and 10 wide. The eyes are 28 inches wide. The nose is nearly 4 feet long. The head is 14 feet high. The top of the figure is higher than the steeple of Trinity Church. The pedestal was built by popular subscriptions raised almost wholly through the efforts of the NEW-YORK WORLD. The statue and pedestal cost $1,000,000. Bedloe's Island is reached from the Grand Union Hotel by the Third-avenue Elevated Road to the Battery, where a small steamboat starts every hour from the Barge Office, and makes the excursion in an hour. The fare for the round trip is twenty-five cents. Pleasant views are afforded of the inner harbor, the Narrows, Governor's Island and its forts, Staten Island, the Brooklyn Bridge, and lower New York. The boat usually lies at the island-wharf long enough for one to walk briskly up to the pedestal, and look off from its upper balustrade, gaining an enchanting view over the lower harbor and its environing cities. Or you can spend a full hour on the island, visiting also the fortifications and barracks of the United-States Artillery, and return on the next boat. The statue is the largest bronze statue in the world, and can be clearly made out from tne Battery and many distant points. It faces very nobly toward the

Narrows, the route from Europe. Inside the sea-wall is an earth-work.

Obelisk, in Central Park, was erected in the Temple of On, in Egypt, about 3,500 years ago, by Thutmes III., King of Egypt, and conqueror of Central Africa, Palestine, and Mesopotamia, with hie-roglyphics illustrating his campaigns and titles, and those of his descendant, Rameses II. For many centuries it stood before the Temple of the Sun, at Heliopolis, and was removed during the reign of Tiberius to Alexandria, where it remained until 1877, when the Khedive, Ismail Pasha, presented it to the city of New York. It was skilfully transported hither by Lieut.-Com. Gorringe, U.S.N., and now stands on the knoll near the Metropolitan Museum of Art, in Central Park. The entire cost of its transportation and setting-up was borne by the late William H. Vanderbilt. It is of granite, 70 feet long, and weighs 200 tons. This noble monument was made before the siege of Troy or the foundation of Rome, and while the Israelites were enslaved in Egypt.

Beethoven, erected in 1884, on the Mall at Central Park. A colos-sal bronze bust, by Baerer, on high granite pedestal. Given by the Männerchor, a German singing society.

Bolivar, the Liberator of South America, has a bold equestrian statue in Central Park, near West 81st Street, dedicated in 1884. It was given to the American people by the Republic of Venezuela.

Burns stands in bronze, on the Mall at Central Park, designed by John Steele, and presented in 1880 by the Scottish New-Yorkers.

Columbus, a colossal marble statue by Emma Stebbins, is tempo-rarily in the Arsenal at Central Park. It was given to the city by Marshall O. Roberts, in 1869.

Commerce, an allegorical bronze figure of heroic size, by the French sculptor, Fosquet, stands near the south-west entrance of Central Park. Stephen B. Guion gave it to the city, in 1866.

William E. Dodge, the late eminent merchant, is represented by a bronze statue, erected by the merchants of New York, at Broadway and 36th Street.

Admiral Farragut is commemorated by a noble bronze statue, designed by Augustus St. Gaudens, on Madison Square. The pedestal curves almost into a semicircle, and has marine decorations. The admiral is represented as on the deck of his ship.

Benjamin Franklin, a bronze statue on Printing-house Square, was erected in 1867, at the expense of Capt. De Groot.

Fitz-Greene Halleck, the poet, has a bronze seated statue on the Mall, Central Park, designed by Wilson MacDonald, erected in 1877

Alexander Hamilton's Statue, presented by his son, John C. Hamilton, in 1880, is in Central Park, near the Museum of Art. It is of white Westerly granite.

Humboldt, the celebrated German traveller and scientist, has a large bronze bust in Central Park, near the south-east corner, presented by German New-Yorkers in 1869. It was designed by Professor Blaiser of Berlin.

The Indian Hunter, by J. Q. A. Ward, stands in Central Park, near the Mall. It is of bronze, and has high art-value.

Lafayette, a bronze statue by Bartholdi, is in Union Square. It was presented by French New-Yorkers, in 1876.

Abraham Lincoln, a bronze statue by H. K. Browne, was erected in 1868, in Union Square, by popular subscription.

Mazzini, an heroic bronze bust of the Italian liberator, was erected in 1878, in Central Park, by Italian New-Yorkers.

Professor S. F. B. Morse has a bronze statue, erected by the Telegraph Operators' Association in 1871 in Central Park, near West 72d Street. He was present at its dedication, but died the next year.

The Pilgrim, a picturesquely posed and attired heroic bronze statue, by J. Q. A. Ward, was presented by New-England New-Yorkers, and stands in Central Park, near East 72d Street.

Schiller, a bronze bust in the Ramble at Central Park, was given in 1859, by German New-Yorkers.

Sir Walter Scott, a bronze copy of the celebrated statue on the Scott monument, at Edinburgh, is on the mall, Central Park, on a pedestal of fine Aberdeen granite. It was given in 1871 (the one-hundredth anniversary of Scott's birth), by Scottish New-Yorkers. The poet is represented seated on a rock, with his dog at his feet.

PRODUCE EXCHANGE (page 52).

Seventh Regiment Monument, a bronze statue of a soldier, by J. Q. A. Ward, is in Central Park, near East 72d Street. It commemorates the soldiers of the regiment dead in the Secession war.

William H. Seward, Secretary of State during the Secession war, has a bronze statue by Randolph Rogers, erected in 1876, in Madison Square.

Shakspeare, a bronze statue, by J. Q. A. Ward, placed on the Mall in Central Park in 1872, by the Shakspeare Dramatic Association.

The Still Hunt, by Kemeys, is a crouching American panther on a high ledge of rocks near the Obelisk, in Central Park.

George Washington is commemorated by an heroic equestrian statue, in Union Square. It was designed by H. K. Browne.

Washington also has a colossal statue by J. Q. A. Ward, erected in 1883, before the Sub-Treasury, on Wall Street, where he took the oath as first President, in 1789.

Washington also has a quaint statue, a copy of that by Houdon, erected by the school-children, at Riverside Park.

Daniel Webster has an heroic bronze statue, given by Gordon W. Burnham, in Central Park, near West 72d Street. It was made in Italy, at a cost of $65,000, and stands on a huge block of granite.

Gen. Worth is commemorated by a granite obelisk at Broadway and Fifth Avenue (Madison Square), erected by the city.

Thomas Addis Emmett, in St. Paul's Churchyard.

Gen. Richard Montgomery, in the Broadway end of St. Paul's.

The Martyrs' Monument, in Trinity Churchyard, commemorating he American soldiers who died in British prisons during the Revolution.

Alexander Hamilton's, Albert Gallatin's, Robert Fulton's, and Capt. Lawrence's (of the "Chesapeake"), in Trinity Churchyard.

Capt.-Gen. Petrus Stuyvesant's, in the outer wall of St. Mark's Church.

Horace Greeley, by J. Q. A. Ward, in bronze, sits before the Tribune Office in his editorial chair.

Garibaldi, in Washington Square, sculptured by Turini, and given by the Italian residents.

EXCHANGES AND BOARDS OF TRADE.

THERE are a number of these in New York, but the two most interesting to strangers are the Stock Exchange and Produce Exchange.

Stock Exchange is on Broad Street, near Wall Street. The stranger should not fail to visit the gallery of the Exchange between the hours of ten and three. As the name would indicate, the business of the Exchange is the purchase and sale of stocks, bonds, and securities. The manner in which the brokers transact business is most amusing and extraordinary, and, to the uninitiated, appears to consist of incoherent shouting and violent gesticulation, to which no one seems to pay the least attention. When the market is active, the scene is as though pandemonium had broken loose. A seat in the Exchange now costs twenty-five or thirty thousand dollars. The building is of white marble, and the great hall is handsomely frescoed. The visitors' gallery is entered from Wall Street.

Produce Exchange is, perhaps, the most imposing and impressive building in New York. It is at the foot of Broadway, and fronts on Bowling Green, and is in rich Italian Renaissance architecture, of brick, with a copious use of terra cotta, in medallions, the arms and names of the States, and projecting galley-prows. Above its uppermost long line of round arches rises an immense campanile, covering 40 by 70 feet, and 225 feet high, richly decorated, and nobly dominating lower New York and the bay. The building is 307 by 150 feet in area, and 116 feet high; and the main hall is a noble one, 220 by 144 feet, and 60 feet high. From the visitors' gallery you may look down on the 3,000 members of the Exchange (organized in 1861, and the largest in the world), and see and hear their fierce bargaining. The scene resembles a pitched battle between walls, and without cavalry. Near the gallery are the sumptuous library and reception rooms. Go to the superintendent of the building, and get a pass (without charge) to ascend the tower. The climb is made luxuriously by elevator; and from the summit you see a magnificent and unrivalled bird's-eye view of lower New York, the bay, Staten Island, the shores and blue mountains of New Jersey, Brooklyn, and Long Island. "Not the White Tower, nor the Colonne Napoleon, nor Bunker-hill Monument, offers any thing equal to the urban, rural, and marine scenery presented to the vision." The building rests on 15,437 piles made of sturdy Maine and Nova Scotia trees. It was planned by George B. Fost, and erected between 1881 and 1884. It is entirely fireproof. The flag flying from its tower is the largest ever made, covering 50 by 20 feet. There are nine passenger elevators. The money-vault contains 1,300 safes, and is defended by seven alternate layers of iron and steel. The Exchange cost $3,179,000. "Harper's Magazine" for July, 1886, has a thirty-page illustrated article describing this vast institution. *From the Grand Union Hotel take the Third-avenue Elevated Road, and get off at Hanover Square, and go through Beaver Street to the Exchange.*

Mercantile Exchange has a new brick and granite building at Hudson and Harrison Streets, with a tall tower. There are 800 members, dealing in butter, cheese, eggs, and groceries.

Cotton Exchange has a new and imposing seven-story building of yellow brick on Hanover Square, south of Wall Street. It cost $1,000,000.

Coal and Iron Exchange is a vast and massive building at the corner of Cortlandt and New Church Streets, the headquarters for dealings in these great commodities.

Consolidated Petroleum Exchange and Stock Board, at 62 Broadway, is oftentimes the scene of most exciting commercial hostilities. It has a membership of 3,000, and is about to erect a huge new building.

American Horse Exchange is at Broadway and 50th Street.

Building Exchange is at 59 Liberty Street.

Coffee Exchange is at 66 Beaver Street. It has over 300 members, and sometimes 100,000 bags of coffee are sold here in a day.

Grocers' Exchange is at Wall and Water Streets. Tea and sugar are the chief commodities sold.

Maritime Exchange is in the Produce-Exchange building. Open

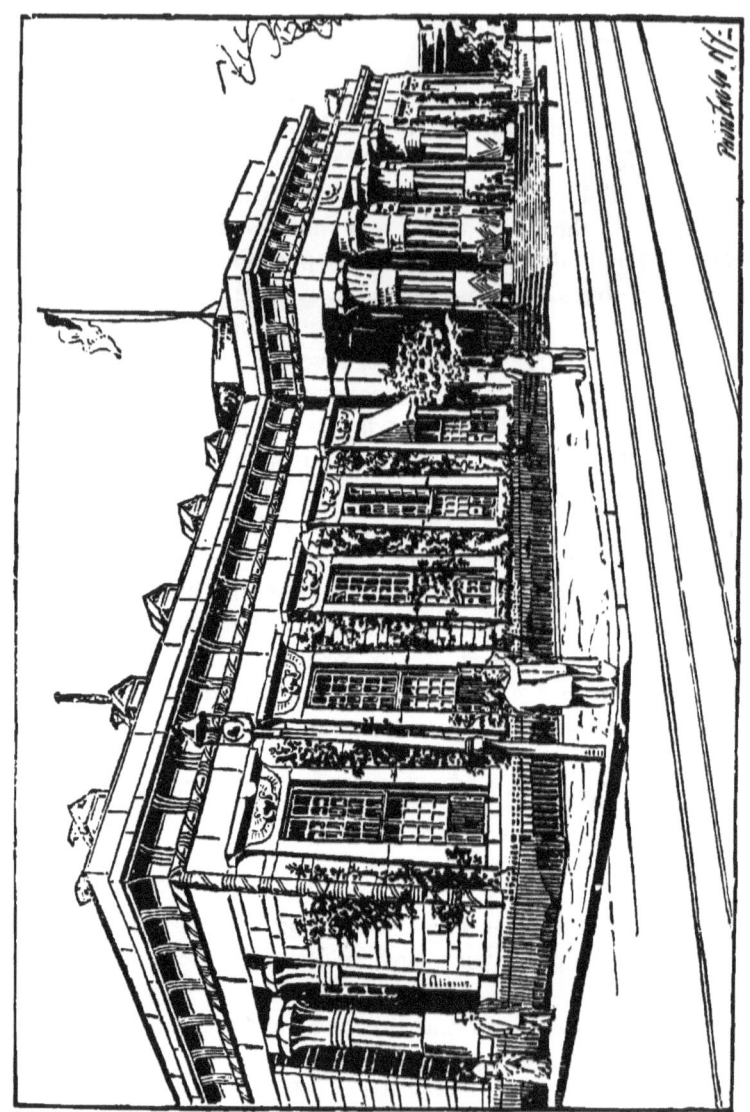

THE "TOMBS" (page 28).

from eight to five (exchange-hours, eleven to three). Marine and commercial news, reading-room, library, etc.

Metal Exchange is at Pearl Street and Burling Slip.

Real-Estate Exchange is at 57 Liberty Street.

American Exchange, 309 Greenwich Street.

Brewers' Exchange, 109 East 15th Street.

Cattle Exchange, Broadway and 38th Street.

Distillers' Wine and Spirit Exchange, 19 South William Street.

Foreign-Fruit Exchange, 64 Broad Street.

Hardware Board of Trade, 6 and 8 Warren Street.

Manhattan Stock Exchange, 69 New Street.

Mechanics' and Traders' Exchange, 289 Fourth Avenue.

Milk Exchange, 6 Harrison Street.

New-York Naval Store and Tobacco Exchange, 113 Pearl Street.

New-York Board of Trade and Transportation, Bryant Building, 55 Liberty Street.

New-York Furniture Board of Trade, Bowery and 150 Canal Street.

New-York Petroleum Exchange and Stock Board, 18 Broadway.

Stationers' Board of Trade, 97 and 99 Nassau Street.

Sugar Exchange, 87 Front Street.

MARKETS.

SOME of the larger markets are worth visiting. The following are the largest : —

Washington Market, bounded by Washington, West, Vesey, and Fulton Streets. This is the largest of the markets, and the principal centre for the distribution of meats and vegetables throughout the city and country.

Fulton Market, bounded by Fulton, Beekman, South, and Front Streets, is also a large market, always containing a fine display of fish, poultry, etc.

At the stands of Eugene G. Blackford, during the first few days of April, there is always a large display of trout from all parts of the country, and at any time of the year the visitor may find a beautiful exhibition of all the obtainable varieties of marine life.

Fulton Fish-Market, opposite Fulton Market, though rather slimy, and always pervaded by "an ancient and fish-like smell," is well worth seeing. Every thing edible that lives in salt water may be seen here. Fish is a cheap and good food, and consequently in great demand.

The other large markets are : —

Catherine, foot of Catherine Street, East River.

Central, East 42d Street, opposite Park Avenue.

Centre, Centre Street, from Grand to Broome.

Clinton, Spring, Canal, West, and Washington Streets.

Essex, Grand Street, from Ludlow to Essex.

Jefferson, Greenwich and Sixth Avenues and West 10th Street.

Gansevoort Market, West, Little 12th, Washington, and Gansevoort Streets.

Tompkins, Third Avenue, between 6th and 7th Streets.

Union, Houston and 2d Streets, and Avenue D.

COLLEGES AND SCHOOLS.

THE city has 300 free public schools, where nearly 4,000 teachers instruct more than 300,000 children, at an annual cost of almost $4,000,000. Children between eight and fourteen are compelled by law to go to school, and twelve truant officers look out for them. There are also many scores of private and parochial schools in the city.

Columbia College occupies an irregular group of brick buildings on the square between Madison and Fourth Avenues and 49th and 50th Streets, near the Cathedral and the Grand Central Depot. It has no dormitories. The chief buildings are the School of Mines, along 50th Street (four-years' course; founded in 1864); the School of Arts, along Madison Avenue (four-years' course; fee, $150 a year; 274 students); the Law School, founded in 1858, and probably the leading one in America (two-years' course ; $150 a year; 397 students) ; and the Library (Geo. H. Baker, librarian), a handsome building, containing 70,000 volumes (open from 8 A.M. to 10 P.M.) in a hall 113 by 75 feet, and 58 feet high. The School of Political Science, opened in 1880 (three-years' course ; fee, $150), is in the School of Arts building ; the School of Medicine is the College of Physicians and Surgeons, at Fourth Avenue and 23d Street. The college has in all 1,600 students ; Seth Low, ex-mayor, is president. It was founded in 1754, as King's College, and largely endowed with land, by Trinity Church. For over a century its buildings were down town, on College Place, between Barclay and Chambers Streets. In 1775 the townspeople drove out the second president, Rev. Miles Cooper, an Oxford graduate, and resembling Dryden in face; and he hid in Stuyvesant's house until he could take ship for England. The college was popularly regarded as a nest of Tories, and remained closed (its buildings serving as barracks and military hospital) until 1784, when the Legislature rechristened it Columbia College. Among its professors are

THE SUB-TREASURY (page 27).

Henry Drisler, H. H. Boyesen, C. F. Chandler, J. S. Newberry, John D. Quackenbos, William R. Ware, and J. Ordronaux. Among its early students were John Jay, Alexander Hamilton, Robert R. Livingston, and Gouverneur Morris.

The woman's department now contains nineteen students. The ancient building with old-fashioned columned portico, in the centre of the college group, was once the Deaf and Dumb Asylum, and was bought by the college about thirty years ago, as a nucleus for its new establishment.

University of the City of New York was founded in 1830, and has 65 instructors and 800 students. The classical and scientific departments are free, and occupy (with the law department) a handsome Gothic building on Washington Square. The medical school of the University is near Bellevue Hospital.

College of the City of New York, at Lexington Avenue and 23d Street, has spacious brick buildings, with a library of 40,000 volumes. It has 230 classical students and 330 scientific students, with 36 instructors, and is free to New-York lads. It was founded in 1847 as the New-York Free Academy, and became a college in 1866. It costs the city $140,000 a year.

College of Physicians and Surgeons, connected with Columbia College, was founded in 1807, and has 20 professors and over 600 students. It was formerly at Fourth Avenue and 23d Street, but it now occupies the splendid new quarters provided for it by William H. Vanderbilt, who in 1885 gave it $500,000, which was increased by $250,000 given by his four sons to establish a free clinic and dispensary, and $250,000 given by his daughter, Mrs. William D. Sloane, to establish the Sloane Maternity Hospital. These new buildings are near Ninth and Tenth Avenues, and 59th and 60th Streets, close by the Roosevelt Hospital and Central Park.

Bellevue-Hospital Medical College was founded in 1861, and has 500 students and a high reputation. It is on the grounds of Bellevue Hospital.

General Theological Seminary of the Protestant-Episcopal Church occupies the block between Ninth and Tenth Avenues, and 20th and

21st Streets. It was founded in 1819, and has 6 professors and 100 students, a three-years' course, a library of 20,000 volumes, and a group of picturesque buildings. It occupies the site of the Chelsea farm, which was made a billet for Hessian officers in 1776. It afterwards belonged to Bishop Moore, and his son, Clement C. Moore.

Union Theological Seminary of the Presbyterian Church was founded in 1836, and occupies a group of handsome new buildings on Lenox Hill, on Park Avenue, between 69th and 70th Streets. Its library contains 50,000 volumes and as many pamphlets, including many rare old books and *incunabula*. Among its professors have been Edward Robinson, W. G. T. Shedd, Henry B. Smith, William Adams, Joel Parker, Philip Schaff, and R. D. Hitchcock (now its president). The property of the Seminary is valued at $2,000,000. The buildings along the avenue are the Morgan Library, the tower-adorned Adams Chapel, and Jessup Hall. Back of these is the great Dormitory. The Chaldaic, Arabic, and Assyrian languages are taught here.

Normal College, on East 69th Street, near Lexington Avenue, is a conventual-looking building of vast extent, with thirty recitation-rooms, lecture-halls, libraries, gymnasia, etc., where 1,600 bright New-York girls are thoroughly educated, and prepared to be school-teachers. The building cost nearly $500,000, and its annual expense to the city is $100,000.

Christian Brothers have nearly a score of great schools in the city, including Manhattan College, at Manhattanville ; the Cathedral School, in 50th Street, with 800 pupils ; the Immaculate-Conception School, in East 14th Street ; the De La Salle Institute, at 48 2d Street ; and the new Catholic high-school, established in the old Charlier Institute.

College of Pharmacy, at 115 West 68th Street, has 5 professors, 300 students, and a two-years' course.

United-States Medical College, eclectic. 239 East 14th Street.

St. John's College, Fordham, Jesuit ; 200 students.

St. Francis Xavier College, West 15th Street, near 5th Avenue ; Jesuit ; 450 students.

Academy of the Sacred Heart, Manhattanville, in a fine wooded park.

overlooking the Hudson River; 200 pupils.   Stone buildings.   Two great dormitories.

Catholic High School.—Christian Brothers.   In the old Charlier-Institute building, near Central Park.

Rutgers Female Institute, 58 West 55th Street.

Friends' Seminary, 226 East 16th Street.

Riding Academy, 8th Avenue and 59th Street, with the largest ring in the world.   Also, Dickel's, 56th Street, near 6th Avenue; Antony's, 5th Avenue and 85th Street; Cohen's, 7th Avenue and 58th Street.

FERRIES.

To	From	Every
Astoria	92d St. E. R.	15 minutes.
Bay Ridge	Whitehall St. E. R.	10 "
Bedloe's Island	U. S. Barge Office, Battery	2 hours.
Brooklyn (Main St.)	Catherine St. E. R.	10 minutes.
" (Fulton St.)	Fulton St. E. R.	5 "
" (Atlantic St.)	Whitehall. E. R.	12 "
" (Hamilton Ave.)	Whitehall. E. R.	10 "
" (Montague St.)	Wall St. E. R.	10 "
" E.D. (Broadway)	Roosevelt St. E. R.	10 "
" " (Grand St.)	Houston St. E. R.	10 "
" " (Broadway)	Grand St. E. R.	7 "
" " (Grand St.)	Grand St. E. R.	12 "
" " (Broadway)	East 23d St. E. R.	12 "
College Point	East 99th St. E. R.	12 "
Communipaw	Liberty St. N. R.	15 "
Fort Lee	129th St. N. R.	30 "
Governor's Island	The Battery	60 "
Greenpoint	East 10th and East 22d Sts. E. R.	10 "
Hoboken	Barclay and Christopher Sts. N.R.	10 "
Hoboken (14th St.)	West 14th St. N. R.	15 "
Hunter's Point	James Slip, 7th and 34th Sts. E. R.	15-30 "
Jersey City	Desbrosses St. N. R.	10 "
Jersey City	Cortlandt St. N. R.	10 "
Jersey City (Pavonia)	Chambers or 23d St. N. R.	10 "
Jersey City (Communipaw)	Liberty St. N. R.	10 "
Staten Island	Whitehall. N. R.	25-45 "
Weehawken	West 42d St. N. R.	15 "

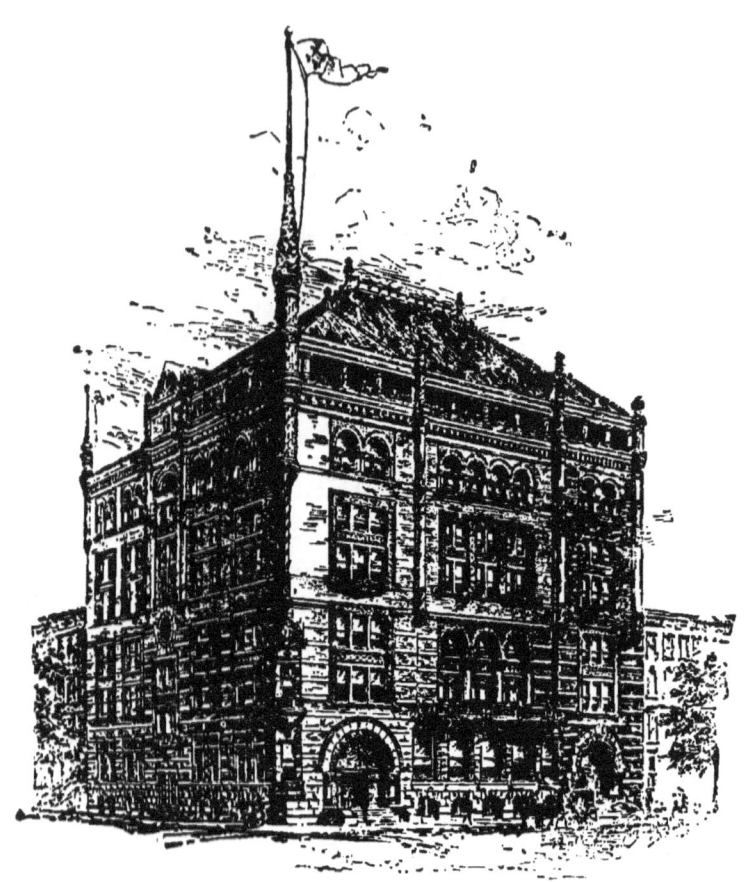

NEW MANHATTAN ATHLETIC CLUB (page 82).

LIBRARIES, ETC.

Free Circulating Library is intended to become to New York what the Public Library is to Boston, except that it will be composed of many separate collections, in different parts of the city. Andrew Carnegie, John Jacob Astor, and others have lately given considerable sums for this purpose. The branches now in operation are at 49 Bond Street (13,000 volumes), and the *Ottendorfer Library*, at 135 Second Avenue, founded by Oswald Ottendorfer in 1884 (12,000 volumes, half of them German). The *Bruce Library* (endowed by Miss Catherine W. Bruce as a memorial of her father) was erected on West 42d Street, west of Seventh Avenue, adjoining the Baptist Church. Another, on Jackson Square, is the gift of Geo. W. Vanderbilt.

Apprentices' Library, founded in 1820, and still conducted by the General Society of Mechanics and Tradesmen, is at 18 East 16th Street. It contains 84,000 volumes, one-third of which are stories. It is free to all without restriction, and circulates 250,000 volumes a year. It is open from 8 A.M. to 9 P.M.

Astor Library, on Lafayette Place, is a handsome brown-stone Romanesque building, 200 feet long, containing 300,000 volumes, and open from 9 A.M. to 5 P.M. (4 in winter). Books are not allowed to go out. There is a spacious vestibule, with 24 marble busts; and of the three great halls above, the centre one is for catalogues and delivery, and the others for general reading. Some of the departments of literature are more complete than in any other American library, and many scholars haunt the twilight alcoves while making books. John Jacob Astor left $400,000 to found the library withal, in 1848; to which his son, William B. Astor, added $550,000; and his grandson, John Jacob Astor, $300,000. There are many Greek and Latin MSS., black-letter volumes, and Shakspeareana.

Cooper Union, a huge brown-stone building at the head of the Bowery, covers an entire square, and contains free libraries, reading-rooms, lecture-foundations, evening schools of design, engraving, science, telegraphy, etc., and the rooms of the American Geographical Society. It was founded by Peter Cooper, a wealthy iron-founder and glue-manufacturer, who stated his ideas thus: "The duty of a business man is to make money : the duty of a Christian is to spend it." He erected this building, in 1857, at a cost of $630,000, and richly endowed the group of free schools that he founded here. The library contains 20,000 volumes.

Mercantile Library, in Clinton Hall, Astor Place, was incorporated in 1866, and is open from 8 A.M. to 9 P.M. It contains 210,000 volumes, and has a large reading-room. There are 5,500 members, who pay $4 or $5 each per year. It has branches at 426 Fifth Avenue and 120 Broadway. A fine library building has recently replaced old Clinton Hall.

Lenox Library is a noble building of white Lockport limestone, in modern French architecture, fronting on Central Park, at Fifth Avenue and 71st Street, 192 by 114 feet in area, forming a court-yard between the central building, its advancing wings, and a ponderous limestone wall with iron gates. It was built and equipped, at a cost of $1,-000.000, by the late James Lenox, who afterwards richly endowed it, for the people. Access to its treasures has not been made so easy for the people, and there have been ferocious skits in the newspapers about the practical exclusion of the public, and as a result, the library is now open, free, to the public from 11 A.M. to 4 P.M., except Sunday and Monday. From the Grand Union Hotel, go up on the Third-avenue Elevated Railroad to 67th-street Station. In the south wing is the library, containing precious *incunabula ;* a perfect Mazarin Bible, printed by Gutenberg and Faust, in 1650, and the oldest of printed books ; Latin Bibles printed at Mayence in 1462 (by Faust and Schöffer), and at Nuremberg in 1477 (with many notes in Melanchthon's handwriting) ; seven fine Caxtons ; block-books ; five of Eliot's Indian Bibles ; "The Recuyell of the Historyes of Troye" (Bruges, 1474), the first book printed in English ; the Bay Psalm Book (Cambridge, 1640), the first book printed in the United States, etc. There are also many rare MSS. on vellum, illuminated, dating from before the invention of printing. These objects are exhibited and entertainingly explained by the accomplished successor of the late Dr. S. Austin Allibone. The picture-gallery is described in chapter on ART.

New-York Historical Society, 170 Second Avenue (open from 9 to 6), has upwards of 70,000 volumes, especially Americana and genealogy. It is inaccessible to the public.

Bar Association (7 West 29th Street) has a library of 24,000 volumes; open to members and the judges.

City Library, 12 City Hall, 10 A.M. to 4 P.M.

American Institute, 115 West 38th Street, 9 to 9.

Masonic, Sixth Avenue and 23d Street.

Mott Memorial (medical), 64 Madison Avenue, open 11 to 9.

New-York Society, 67 University Place, 8 to 6, 70,000 volumes. Founded 1754; $15 a year.

New-York Law-Institute Library, 116 Post-office Building. Open 9 A.M. to 5 P.M.; 30,000 legal works.

Young Men's Christian Association has several libraries in different localities.

American Museum of Natural History, between Eighth and Ninth Avenues, and 77th and 81st Streets, was founded in 1869. The corner-stone of this building was laid by President Grant in 1874, and the Museum was opened in 1877 by President Hayes. It is a Gothic building of brick and granite, with several large and admirably arranged halls. Here are found the Powell collection of British-Columbian objects, the Robert-Bell collection from Hudson's Bay, the De-Morgan collection of stone-age implements from the valley of the Somme, the Jesup collection of North-American woods and building stones, the James-Hall collections in paleontology and geology, the Gay collection of shells, the Bailey collection of birds' nests and eggs, mounted mammalia, Indian dresses and weapons, Pacific-Islanders' implements and weapons, 10,000 mounted birds, the Major-Jones collection of Indian and mound-builders' antiquities from Georgia, the

Porto-Rico antiquities, a mammoth twenty-five feet high; several specimens of the extinct Australian bird, the Moa, fifteen feet high; reptiles, fishes, corals, minerals, etc. The library contains 12,000 scientific works. Many lectures are given here yearly for the teachers in the public schools, who come here to study these vast and interest-ing collections. New buildings are about to be added by the State. The Museum is open free on Wednesdays, Thursdays, Fridays, and Saturdays. It is reached by the Sixth-avenue Elevated Railroad to the 81st-street Station, or by the Eighth-avenue horse-cars.

Grand Central Depot, the largest and finest passenger station in America, is located on Forty-second Street, directly opposite the Grand Union Hotel. It is used jointly by the New York Central and Hudson River Railroad, the Harlem Railroad, and the New York. New Haven and Hartford Railroad, with the connections of the latter ramifying all over New England.

CHURCHES.

THERE are about 400 churches in New York, capable of seating at one time 250,000 persons, and valued at $60,000,000.

ROMAN CATHOLIC. — There are 75 Roman-Catholic churches in New York, representing a vast population, as each has several different congregations on each day of worship. Several of the churches are German, Polish, etc.

St. Patrick's Cathedral is the greatest and most magnificent church in the United States. It was projected in 1850 by Archbishop Hughes, and the plans drawn by James Renwick. The corner-stone was laid in 1858, in the presence of 100,000 persons; and May 25, 1879, the cathedral was dedicated by Cardinal McCloskey. It has cost over $2,000,000. It is in thirteenth-century decorated Gothic, like the cathedrals of Amiens, Cologne, York, and Exeter; and the material is fine white marble. It is a Latin cross, 306 feet long, and 120 feet wide (140 at transepts), and 108 feet high, with a noble clerestory upheld on long lines of clustered marble columns, and carrying a lofty and richly ornamented ceiling. On each side of the front gable (which is 156 feet high, or taller than most of the steeples of America), the carved and pinnacled spires reach the great height of 328 feet, making a huge marble mountain, uplifted on the highest point of Fifth Avenue, truly a landmark for leagues. The 70 windows (37 of which are memorial) are of rich stained glass, and were made at Chartres, France, at a cost of $100,000. That in the south transept shows forth the life of St. Patrick; that in the north, the life of the Blessed Virgin. The main altar is 40 feet high, of Italian marble, inlaid with gems, and bass-reliefs of the Passion; and on one side is the great Gothic throne of the archbishop. The altar of the Holy Family, of Tennessee marble and Caen stone; of the Blessed Virgin, of curiously carved French walnut; of the Sacred Heart, of bronze; of St. Joseph, of bronze and mosaic, — are all of great interest and artis

TRINITY CHURCH.

tic merit. High mass is given at 10.30 A.M., on Sunday, and vespers at 4 P.M. The cathedral is open every day of the week. Seats in the centre may be had at high mass for 25 cents (on the sides for 15 cents), tickets being procured from the verger near the main entrance, inside.

St. Paul the Apostle, at 60th Street and Ninth Avenue, pertains to the celebrated preaching Order of Paulists, whose monastery adjoins it. It is an immense and sombre pile of gray stone, with an ascetic interior, singularly devoid of ornament, but impressive from its great size. The main portals are flanked by statues of the saints.

St. Patrick's, at Mott and Prince Streets, erected in 1815, and with a very spacious interior, was formerly the cathedral.

Church of the Most Holy Redeemer (German), at 30th Street and Avenue A, is a rich Byzantine building, with lofty roof, costly altar, and a spire 265 feet high.

St. Stephen's, on East 28th Street, near Third Avenue, is celebrated for its beautiful music. This was the church of the famous Dr. McGlynn.

St. Francis Xavier is on West 16th Street, near Sixth Avenue.

St. Ann's is at 112 East 12th Street.

St. Mary's is at 438 Grand Street.

St. Vincent de Paul's is a French church, on West 23d Street.

EPISCOPALIAN. — There are 76 churches of this sect in New York, of which the following may be distinguished: —

Trinity Church, on Broadway, at the head of Wall Street, is the richest parish in America, having revenues of $500,000 a year. It was founded in 1697, receiving from the English Government a grant of its present site, outside the north gate of the city, to which in 1705 was added Queen Anne's Farm, including the territory along the river from Vesey Street to Christopher Street. Much of this great domain remains in the possession of the parish. Other singular resources were added to Trinity's store. It received a fund raised for relieving Christian slaves out of Salee; was granted all wrecks and drift-whales on the island of Nassau; Jewish citizens contributed for its spire; and the Widow Hellegard DeKay loaned it £400. Communion services were given by William and Mary, Queen Anne, and King George. Among the rectors were Dr. Vesey, for 50 years; Dr. Barclay, from 1746 to 1764; Dr. Auchmuty; Bishops Provoost, Moore, and Hobart; Dr. Hobart. When the Revolution broke out, the clergy were Royalist; and the patriots closed the church, which was burned down in 1776, and rebuilt in 1788. The present church dates from 1846, and is a noble Gothic structure, with a rich gray interior, carved Gothic columns, groined roofs, and the magnificent marble and mosaic altar and reredos, erected by his family as a memorial to the late William B. Astor. The church is usually open all day long, throughout the week, with morning and evening prayers, at 9 A.M. and 3 P.M., and imposing choral services on Sunday. The parish spends enormous sums annually in charities. Upjohn, the greatest of American architects in the Gothic style, devoted seven years to building Trinity. It has an elaborate chancel service of silver, presented by good Queen Anne. Its spire, 284 feet high, commands a wide and wonderful view, and contains a melodious chime of bells.

St. Paul's, at Broadway and Vesey Street, was built in 1764-66, and faces away from Broadway, and was attended by Washington. It is a chapel of Trinity parish. The interior is quaint and old-fashioned to a degree. At mid-aisle, on the Vesey-street side, the site of the pew of Washington is marked with his initials. The organ was brought from England long years ago. Dr. Auchmuty used to read prayers for the king, in the chancel, until the drummers of the American garrison beat him down with the long roll in the centre aisle.

Among those buried in St. Paul's churchyard were Emmet and MacNeven, Irish patriots of '98; Gen. Richard Montgomery, the brave Irish-American, who was killed in storming Quebec; John Dixey, R.A., an Irish sculptor; Capt. Baron de Rahenan, of one of the old Hessian regiments; Col. the Sieur de Rochefontaine, of our Revolutionary army; John Lucas and Job Sumner, majors in the Georgia Line and Massachusetts Line; and Lieut.-Col. Beverly Robinson, the Loyalist.

Trinity Chapel is a brown-stone Gothic church, on 25th Street, close to Madison Square. The inside walls are of Caen stone, with tiled floors, and rich stained windows.

St. John's is a venerable sandstone chapel of Trinity parish, with a deep portico, on St. John's Park, where the great New-York Central freight-station now stands. Rev. P. A. H. Brown is rector.

St. Augustine's, in Houston Street, near the Bowery, is a handsome Queen Anne chapel of Trinity, with industrial schools, guilds, and mission-house. Dr. Kimber is in charge. An illuminated crystal cross on its lofty spire indicates when services are being held. The bell was cast in 1700, and presented by the Bishop of London, in 1704.

Grace Church looks down Broadway from 10th Street, and is a very sumptuous and ornate edifice of marble, with a lofty marble spire. The interior is rich in delicate carvings, lines of stone columns, forty stained-glass windows, etc. Renwick built the church in 1845. Dr. Huntington is rector. You should visit the beautiful little chantry, opening off the south aisle, and erected by Catherine Wolf's bounty.

Calvary Church, at Fourth Avenue and 21st Street, is a cathedral-like stone structure, with a rich and spacious interior, great transepts, and clustered Gothic columns. It dates from 1847.

St. George's, Low-church, on Stuyvesant Square, is an immense Byzantine structure of brown-stone, with lofty twin-spires, a rich chancel, and brilliant polychromatic interior. The elder Dr. Stephen H. Tyng was many years rector. W. S. Rainsford is rector.

St. Mark's is a quaint old church, at Second Avenue and Stuyvesant Place, with many mural tablets, and the tombs of Petrus Stuyvesant, the last Dutch governor; Col. Slaughter, one of the English governors; and Gov. Tompkins. From the adjacent church-yard, A. T. Stewart's body was stolen, by night. On the site of St. Mark's, Gov. Stuyvesant built a chapel, near his quaint yellow-brick house, over two centuries ago.

Church of the Holy Spirit, at Madison Avenue and 66th Street, designed by R. H. Robertson, is famous for its fine wood-carvings.

St. James, on Madison Avenue, corner of 71st Street, is one of the most elegant in the denomination. The new edifice is but a few years old, but it is admired for its graceful exterior and its exquisite interior.

St. Bartholomew's, at Madison Avenue and West 44th Street, has a sumptuous richness of brilliant colors and gold, and stained windows, arcades and round arches, and polished granite pillars.

Church of the Heavenly Rest, at 551 Fifth Avenue, contains polished red and gray granite pillars, with immensely costly capitals, in carved roses and lilies; frescos of Fra Angelico's seraphs; richly carved roof-timbers, and brilliant windows.   Low-church.

St. Ignatius, 56 West 40th Street, opposite Bryant Park, is High-church and ritualistic, with a rich and almost Roman service, largely choral, and a fine marble altar.   Arthur Ritchie is rector.

St. Mary the Virgin is a ritualistic church, at 228 West 45th Street.

Anthon Memorial Church, 781 Madison Ave., Heber Newton, rector.

St. Thomas (Dr. Brown), at Fifth Avenue and West 53d Street, is in Early-English Gothic, with its seven-sided chancel adorned with a magnificent group of paintings by John LaFarge, representing the Adoration of the Cross, with sculptures by Augustus St. Gaudens. The church cost $750,000.

Church of the Holy Trinity, at Madison Avenue and 42d Street, was the place of the younger Dr. Stephen H. Tyng's labors for many years.   It is Low-church in its forms.

PRESBYTERIAN. — Including the Reformed and the United wings, the Presbyterians have 55 churches.

First Presbyterian Church, on Fifth Avenue, near 11th Street, is a handsome stone building.

Madison-Square Church is a neat brown-stone structure.   Dr Parkhurst is pastor.

Brick Church, at Fifth Avenue and 37th Street, w'th a lofty spire. was for many years the scene of Dr. Spring's labors, and belongs to the oldest of the Presbyterian societies, formerly on Beekman Street. Dr. Vandyke is pastor.

University-Place Church, at 10th Street, is of stone, with a spire 184 feet high.

Church of the Covenant, at 34th Street and Park Avenue, is a Lombardo-Gothic temple.

Fifth-Avenue Church, at 708 Fifth Avenue, corner of West 55th Street, is an enormous Gothic structure, with a spire of great height. It cost $750,000. Dr. John Hall, the celebrated English divine, is the pastor.

METHODIST. — There are 66 Methodist churches in New York, 5 of which are German, 6 African, 1 Swedish, and 1 Welsh.

John-Street Church is the cradle of American Methodism, which began in 1766, when Philip Embury preached to four persons. Two years later, the society bought this site, and built the Wesley Chapel, replaced in 1817 and in 1841 by larger churches. The clock now there was presented by John Wesley, and the society has other precious relics of the early days.

St. Paul's, at Fourth Avenue and East 22d Street, is a handsome white-stone structure, in Romanesque architecture, with a spire 210 feet high.

St. Luke's is at 108 West 41st Street.

Asbury Church is at 82 Washington Square.

Lexington-Avenue Church is at East 52d Street.

BAPTISTS have 43 churches, including those for the French, Swedes, Germans, Africans, and other nationalities.

Fifth-Avenue Church is at the corner of West 46th Street. W. II. P. Faunce is the pastor.

Madison-Avenue Church is at the corner of East 31st Street. Dr. Sanders is pastor.

Epiphany is at Madison Avenue and 64th Street. Dr. Beckley.

Calvary Church, on West 57th Street, is ministered to by Dr. MacArthur.

First Baptist Church, at Broome and Elizabeth Streets, is a Gothic building of rough stone.

Tabernacle, on Second Avenue, near 10th Street, is an attractive Gothic building, near St. Mark's.   This was once the leading Baptist church in America, in Dr. Edward Lothrop's day, but having run down, it was on the verge of being sold for a synagogue, until it was revived and beautified by its present pastor, the Rev. Dr. D. G. Potter, largely aided by contributions from the leaders of the Standard Oil Company.

CONGREGATIONALISTS have 8 churches.
Tabernacle, at Sixth Avenue and 34th Street, is a handsome Gothic temple, with elaborately carved pulpit and organ-screen.   Dr. Henry A. Stimson is pastor.
On lower Madison Avenue, there are two Congregational churches, at East 45th Street and East 47th Street.

UNIVERSALISTS maintain 4 churches.
Church of the Divine Paternity (Dr. Eaton), at Fifth Avenue and 45th Street, was for many years ministered to by Dr. E. H. Chapin.   It has towers 185 feet high.

UNITARIANS support 2 churches, widely known by reason of their illustrious pastors.
All Souls' Church, at Fourth Avenue and East 20th Street, is a quaint red-and-white Byzantine edifice, in the style of the mediæval Italian churches, in which the late Dr. Bellows preached for many years.   Dr. Williams is pastor.
Church of the Messiah, at Park Avenue and East 34th Street, on Murray Hill, is a spacious and handsome structure, with a beautiful portal.   Robert Collyer is pastor.

REFORMED DUTCH have 24 churches and chapels.
Collegiate Middle Reformed Church, at 4th Street and Lafayette Place, built in 1839, has a handsome marble pulpit and a fine interior.
Other Reformed Churches are on Fifth Avenue, at 21st, 29th, and 48th Streets.   The latter is a rich and florid Gothic building of brown-stone, with colored windows, many high gables, and flying buttresses

HEBREW. — There are 40 synagogues and temples, with strange Oriental names and ritual, and many smaller shrines.

Temple Emanu-El, at Fifth Avenue and West 43d Street, is a picturesque pile of Oriental architecture, erected at a cost of $650,000, and rich in delicate detail-work, carvings, and color. The interior is dazzling in its brilliancy.

SMALLER SECTS of every conceivable character have churches or meeting-places in various localities. Some of these are, —

Catholic Apostolic, 417 West 57th Street.
Christian Israelites, 108 1st Street.
Reformed Episcopal, Madison Avenue and 55th Street. (Dr. Sabine.)
New Jerusalem, 114 East 35th Street. (Mr. Seward.)
Reformed Catholic, 79 West 23d Street.
Moravian, 154 Lexington Avenue.
Friends, 124 East 20th Street, 43 West 47th Street, and East 15th Street, and Rutherford Place.
Lutheran, 216 East 15th Street.

RESIDENCE OF MRS. WM. H. VANDERBILT (page 102).

THE CITY HALL (page 25).

THEATRES.

THE theatres of New York are among the best in the world, and should be visited by every sojourner in the tents of Manhattan. Care should be taken about buying tickets from speculators outside, as in some of the theatres such tickets will not be accepted.

The sidewalks on Union Square, near the Washington statue, are frequented by numbers of actors waiting for engagements, and has hence come to be known as "The Slave Market," and "The Rialto."

Several of the leading theatres, including the Metropolitan Opera House, the Casino, and the Standard, are on Broadway, within half a mile of the Grand Union Hotel. All the others are of easy and quick access from the hotel.

Academy of Music, a long and plain brick building at the corner of 14th Street and Irving Place, has been, since 1866, the home of Italian opera in New York, and latterly of Denman Thompson's famous "Old Homestead." It cost $360,000, and has a magnificent interior, where some of the most notable balls and other entertainments have taken place. Amberg's Theatre, nearly opposite, covers the site of old Irving Hall. The Academy has heard the impassioned songs of Lucca, Nilsson, Kellogg, Tietjens, Piccolomini, Gerster, Hauk, Brignoli, Campanini, Mario, and other famous singers.

Abbey's Theatre is on the corner of Broadway and 38th Street.

American, Eighth Avenue and 42d Street.

Bijou Opera-House, on Broadway, between 30th and 31st Streets, is the home of light farce and burlesque.

Casino, at Broadway and 39th St., is a beautiful Moorish structure, modelled after parts of the famous Alhambra. Here are produced comic operas, musical extravaganzas, and other light amusements. On the roof is a pleasant and popular *café* and summer-garden.

Columbus, East 125th Street, near Lexington Avenue.

Daly's, at Broadway and 31st Street, has an admirable stock company, and renders modern and classic English comedies in a style of incomparable excellence.   Augustin Daly is its manager.

Empire, Broadway and 40th Street.

Fifth-Avenue Theatre, corner of Broadway and 28th Street, is a beautiful and successful "star" theatre, built for Augustin Daly, and now managed by Harry Miner.

Fourteenth-Street Theatre, on 14th Street, near Sixth Avenue, is a handsome gray building, with a classic portico.   It has also been known as the Lyceum Theatre (when Fechter conducted it), and Haverly's.   It has a very handsome and comfortable auditorium.

Garrick, 35th Street, near Sixth Avenue.

Garden, Madison Avenue and 27th Street.

Grand Opera-House, at Eighth Avenue and 23d Street, is an immense structure of white marble, for a long time run by James Fisk, jun.   The prices here are much lower than at the other large theatres, and its great auditorium has witnessed many fine "star" performances.

Herald Square Theatre, at Broadway and 35th Street, furnishes capital novelties and comedies, including many of the leading attractions.

Harry Miner's Theatres, one on Eighth Avenue, near 23d Street, and the other on the Bowery, near Broome Street, are devoted to varieties and other light performances.

Hoyt's, West 24th Street, near Broadway.

Irving Place, East 15th Street and Irving Place.

London Theatre, on the Bowery, between Rivington and Stanton Streets, produces varieties and popular shows.

Lyceum Theatre is a beautiful new structure on Fourth Avenue, near 23d Street (next to the Academy of Design), built under the direction of Steele Mackaye, and richly decorated by Tiffany.   Here one may see modern comedies and popular dramas of high excellence.

Madison-Square Garden, at Fourth and Madison Avenues, and 26th and 27th Streets, has the largest auditorium in the city.

Metropolitan Opera-House is one of the largest theatres in the world, and has 122 boxes (each with a spacious parlor attached), and seats for 6,000 persons. It is an enormous Renaissance building, of yellow brick, 200 by 260 feet, with broad foyers, 17 entrances, and a stage 96 by 76 feet, and 120 feet high. The structure is of brick and iron, and practically fireproof. It was opened in 1883, by Nilsson and Campanini, in " Faust." Here the great German and Italian operas are given in magnificent style, with every accessory of fine scenery and stage-effects. It fronts on Broadway, and extends from 38th to 39th Streets.

Oriental Theatre, 113 Bowery, gives performances in Hebrew.

Proctor's, West 23d Street, near Sixth Avenue.

People's Theatre is at 199 Bowery.

Standard Theatre, at Broadway, Sixth Avenue, and 33d Street, is a large new theatre, devoted to modern society plays, comedies, etc.

Star Theatre, at Broadway and 13th Street, has a large and brilliant auditorium, devoted to high class and " star " representations. It is the old Wallack's Theatre.

Thalia Theatre, at 46 Bowery (corner of Canal Street), is devoted to plays in Hebrew, given at odd intervals. It occupies the site of the famous old Bowery Theatre, opened in 1826, and notable for the triumphs of Forrest, Rice, Junius Brutus Booth, Charlotte Cushman, and other great actors.

Tony Pastor's Theatre, on East 14th Street, between Tammany Hall and the Academy of Music, is sacred to variety shows, and is the best of its kind in the city.

Union-Square Theatre, at 56 East 14th Street, near Broadway, is a handsome little house, always a favorite with theatre-goers, where the best " star " actors make their appearance. Take Third-avenue Elevated Railroad to 14th Street.

Palmer's (Broadway and 30th Street) is one of the leading theatres of the metropolis, presenting the best attractions in the country, and a brilliant and comfortable auditorium. It presents choice modern dramas and comedies, in a style of great splendor. The manager is A. M. Palmer, who also controls the Madison-Square Theatre.

Public Halls. At Chickering Hall (Fifth Avenue and 18th Street), Hardman Hall (2 West 19th Street, cor. Fifth Avenue), and other large and beautifully decorated halls, lectures and concerts and other fashionable public entertainments are given frequently.

Eden Musée, on West 23d Street, near Fifth Avenue, is an attractive new building, containing wax portrait-figures of many famous men and women, in life-size, historical groups, a subterranean Chamber of Horrors, and other interesting curiosities. Almost all visitors to New York include this remarkably instructive and entertaining sight in their grand rounds. The entrance-fee is fifty cents ; and the collection is one of the very best and largest of the kind in the world, rivalling the famous London wax-works of Madame Tussaud.

Harlem Opera-House, built and managed by Oscar Hammerstein, is on 125th Street, near Seventh Avenue, and is one of the most charming theatres in the city. It is devoted chiefly to light opera.

Broadway Theatre, at Broadway and 41st Street, is a very handsome new theatre, and is said to be fire-proof. It is devoted to light opera of the better class, and rivals the Casino in popularity. It is open all summer.

Base Ball may be seen at the Polo Grounds, Eighth Avenue and 155th Street. Reached by Sixth-avenue Elevated Railroad to 155th Street.

Manhattan Athletic Club grounds, Eighth Avenue and 56th Street. Sixth-avenue Elevated Railroad to 53d-street Station.

Caledonian Club, foot of E. 68th Street, at Jones's Wood. Second-avenue Elevated Railroad to 65th-street Station.

New-York Athletic Club's grounds, Travers Island, near New Rochelle.

Shops and Theatres.

All the large retail shops and the leading theatres are within a few minutes' walk or ride of the Grand Union Hotel.

CLUBS, SOCIETIES, ETC.

Union League Club house, at Fifth Avenue and West 39th Street,
was built in 1879–80, at a cost of $400,000, with sumptuous halls, din-
ing-room, art-gallery, library, billiard-room, *café*, etc., decorated by
Louis Tiffany, John LaFarge, and Franklin Smith. The club has
1,500 members. The entrance-fee is $300, and the annual dues $75.
It was organized in 1863, as a union of gentlemen devoted to "abso-
lute and unqualified loyalty to the Government of the United States
. . . to resist and expose corruption, and promote reform in National,
State, and municipal affairs ; and to elevate the idea of American
citizenship." It raised and equipped several regiments for the National armies during the Secession war. This is the most elegant
club-house in America.

Union Club is a prominent social organization at Fifth Avenue and
21st Street.

Authors' Club, at 158 West 23d St., decorated by Francis Lathrop,
is the haunt of the leading men of letters in the great metropolis.
Among its members are Curtis, Eggleston, Stedman, Stoddard, Bun-
ner, Matthews, Boyesen, Godwin, Hay, and James. In the same building is the hall of the New-York Fencing Club (see CENTURY MAGA-
ZINE, January, 1887).

Grolier Club (29 East 32d Street) contains 50 bibliophiles, and
studies bookbinding, extending, fine printing, paper-making, etc., as
arts.

New-York Athletic Club, founded in 1868, is the leading society of
the kind in America. It has a four-story building at Sixth Avenue
and 55th Street, with bowling, billiards, swimming-tanks, gymnasium,
café, parlors, reading-room, etc. The grounds and boat-houses are at
Travers Island. There are 2.000 members.

New Manhattan Athletic Club (45th St. and Madison Avenue) has a
sumptuous establishment of stone and brick for its home, with *café*,

billiard, chess, and card rooms, reading-room, and great wealth of statuary, paintings, velvet carpets, gymnasium, etc. Their athletic grounds and cinder-track are at Eighth Avenue and 56th and 57th Streets. The club was founded in 1877.

Lotos Club, at Fifth Avenue and 21st Street, is a social organization, with monthly art-receptions in its handsome brown-stone building. It includes many authors. artists, actors, etc. Admission, $200 ; annual dues, $50. There are 500 members.

Century Association, in West 43d Street, is for the advancement of literature and art, and has a fine library and picture-gallery. 600 members.

Caledonian Club, handsome sandstone building at Greenwich Avenue and 13th Street (Jackson Square). Founded in 1856, as a social and athletic society for Scotchmen.

Calumet Club, 267 Fifth Avenue. Young society-men.

Canadian Club, 12 East 29th Street. Founded 1884.

Coney-Island Jockey Club, 173 Fifth Avenue.

Down-Town Club, 60 Pine Street. 500 members.

Harmonie Club, in a handsome building at 46 West 42d Street. 360 German members. Founded in 1852.

The Lambs, 26 West 31st Street, largely composed of actors. Lester Wallack was the first Shepherd.

Merchants' Club, 337 Broadway. Founded 1872. 200 members.

New-York Press Club, 120 Nassau Street. 350 members. Founded ,1872.

New-York Southern Society includes many eminent Southerners, now domiciled in New York. 18 West 25th Street.

Racquet Club, 43d Street, near Fifth Avenue. Four courts. 450 members.

Kit-Kat Club, 12 East 15th Street, is composed of artists.

Knickerbocker Club, at Fifth Avenue and 32d Street, is a very aristocratic society of 300 members.

Manhattan Club has its home in the Stewart palace, Fifth Avenue and 34th Street. It was founded in 1865, to advance Democratic principles.

St. Nicholas Club, 386 Fifth Avenue, was founded in 1875, as a social organization of descendants of the New-York families prior to 1785. 300 members.

St. Nicholas Society, founded in 1835, for descendants of old New-Yorkers before 1785, has famous dinners, and includes the old aristocracy of the city.

Sorosis is a woman's club, founded in 1868, and now, with 350 members, makes its home at 212 Fifth Avenue.

University Club, Madison Avenue and 26th Street (old Union-League Club-house). Founded in 1865. For former students at college, West Point, or Annapolis.

Tammany Society was founded in 1789, to inculcate love of America, with an aboriginal ritual, intended to conciliate the hostile Indians, and to antagonize the aristocratic Cincinnati. William Mooney was the first Grand Sachem. The members, in Indian costume, received the sachems of the Creeks from Carolina.

Yacht-Clubs. — The Larchmont, New-York (57 Madison Avenue), American (Milton Point, Rye), Seawanhaka (Bay Ridge), and Atlantic (Bay Ridge), are the chief yacht-clubs of the city.

Rowing-Clubs include the Atalanta, Nassau, Gramercy, Columbia-College, and New-York Athletic, which have their boat-houses along Harlem River, near Third Avenue.

Bicycling-Clubs. — The New-York Bicycling Club, founded in 1879, has a home at 146 West-End Avenue. The Citizens' Bicycle Club is at 26 West 60th Street, where they have the best club-house for the purpose in America. Several smaller clubs are in existence. There are upwards of 5,000 bicycles in the city, and great numbers in Brooklyn and other adjacent municipalities.

Ohio Society of New York, 236 Fifth Avenue.

American Chemical Society, University Building.

American Ethnological Society, 35 Pine Street. It dates from 1842, and Albert Gallatin was its first president.

American Geographical Society owns a building at No. 11 West 29th Street. Founded in 1852. 1,500 fellows. Chief Justice Charles P. Daly is president. It has 20,000 volumes and 8,000 maps.

American Meteorological Society, East 49th Street.

American Microscopical Society, East 26th Street. Founded 1865.

American Numismatic and Archœological Society, 17 West 43d St.

American Philological Society, 36 Cooper Union.

New-York Genealogical and Biographical Society, 23 West 44th St.

New-York Horticultural Society, 26 West 28th Street.

Masonic Temple (Sixth Avenue and 23d Street) is a massive and simple building of gray granite, erected at a cost of over $1,000,000. The ground-floor is devoted to business, the second floor to the Grand-Lodge Hall, the third and fourth to lodge and chapter rooms.

Odd-Fellows' Hall, at Grand and Centre Streets, is a singular-looking and massive structure, built about the year 1860, and containing many decorated lodge-rooms. There are about 100 lodges.

Young Men's Christian Association, at Fourth Avenue and 23d Street, has a spacious and stately Renaissance building (erected in 1869) of New-Jersey brown-stone, and yellow Ohio marble; with library (35,000 volumes), gymnasium, lecture-rooms. It is open from 8 A.M. to 10 P.M. (Sundays, 2 to 10), and strangers are made very welcome. It aims to improve the spiritual, mental, and physical condition of young men by evening classes, sociables, prayer-meetings, Bible-classes, music, entertainments, etc. There are seven branches.

Young Women's Christian Association, in East 15th Street, near Fifth Avenue, is a handsome building of red brick and rock-faced Belleville stone, with a pyramidal roof of red Akron tiles, and abundant tiling, terra cotta, oaken wainscots, stained glass, etc. Inside are rich parlors, a large chapel, employment rooms, a large library (10,000 volumes), and free schools for type-writing, book-keeping, short-hand, dress-making, wall-paper designing, modelling, etc.

The Association was founded in 1871, and has 180 members. R. H. Robertson erected the building in 1886, at a cost of $125,000, to which John Jacob Astor gave $30,000, and the three Vanderbilt daughters (Mrs. Sloane, Mrs. Shepard, and Mrs. Twombly) $45,500.

"FLATS," OR APARTMENT-HOUSES.

SOME of the largest and finest structures in the city are the apart-ment-houses, or " flats." Each apartment is complete in itself, con-taining all the rooms requisite for housekeeping. The rent of an apartment of the better class ranges from one to seven thousand dollars per year, according to size and location. The buildings are provided with elevators, hall-boys, electric lights, and in many cases are fire-proof. The expensive apartments are elegantly fitted up with hard-woods and inlaid floors, frescos, etc., and contain from seven to twenty-five rooms each. One of the differences between " Flats " and " Apartment-Houses " is that the former have kitchens, equipped for housekeeping; while the latter have restaurants where the occupants get their meals. The following are among the largest : —

Central-Park Apartment-Houses, on 59th Street, near Seventh Ave-nue, form the largest flat-hotel in the world, including several huge fireproof buildings, — the Madrid, Cordova, Granada, Lisbon, — com-prehended in one plan, and magnificent in all their appointments. The whole structure is best known as the " Navarro Flats," and is said to have cost upwards of seven million dollars.

Dakota, at Eighth Avenue and 72d Street, is another vast and costly structure, 155 feet high, and gorgeous in all its detaisl. It is called the finest in New York. The rent of an apartment runs as high as seven thousand dollars a year. It was built by Clark, of Singer Sewing-Machine fame.

Osborne, at the corner of Seventh Avenue and 57th Street, is 11 stories (171 feet) high, of rock-faced Connecticut brown-stone, fire-proof, with floors and roof of iron, brick, and concrete, all rooms fin-ished in mahogany or ash, electric lights, steam-heat, Tiffany stained glass, etc. The main entrance is said to be the finest in New York, with heavy oaken doors, rare marbles, mosaic, frescos, and stained glass, furnished by the LaFarge Decorative Art Company.

ISLANDS.

Staten Island, at the mouth of the harbor, covers nearly 60 square miles, and has 40,000 inhabitants, two railroads, the Sailors' Snug Harbor (near New Brighton), the summer-resorts at St. George, and the great fortifications overlooking the Narrows. People call it "the American Isle of Wight," on account of the beauty of its scenery of hill and sea; and many New-York merchants have their homes here. It was the *Staaten Eylandt* of the Dutch, and is a county of New York. Ferry-boats leave Whitehall every half-hour or so, for St. George. Fare, ten cents. It has along part of its length the Staten-Island Railroad, which is a connecting chain of many very attractive villages, where are to be seen hundreds of remarkably pretty homes. Here George William Curtis has lived many years. Here, too, lives Erastus Wiman, who of late years has been foremost in advancing the interests of Staten Island.

David's Island, off New Rochelle, was made an army hospital in 1861, and a depot for recruits in 1869. It is now a sort of school for company-cooks for the American army.

Hart's Island, off Pelham Neck, is the site of city hospitals and workhouses, and of the Potter's Field, where over 2,000 pauper and unknown dead are buried every year.

Ward's Island, near Hell Gate, has 200 acres, with fine old forests, and the State Emigrant Hospital, House of Refuge, Lunatic Hospital, Homœopathic Hospital, Soldiers' Home, etc., a group of costly buildings, attractively embowered in foliage, and looking out on wide lawns.

Bedloe's Island, 2 miles from the Battery, covers $13\frac{1}{2}$ acres, and has the obsolete works of Fort Wool, with a small garrison of artillerists, and the Bartholdi statue of Liberty.

Ellis Island, $1\frac{1}{4}$ miles from the Battery, is now the landing place for emigrants. It contains the ancient bulwarks of Fort Gibson.

Randall's Island covers 100 acres, where the Harlem River enters the East River, and has 2,500 inhabitants, mostly destitute children in the House of Refuge, Children's Hospital, Nursery, and other vast and handsome brick buildings, where they are instructed in work and study by the paternal city.

Blackwell's Island, in the East River, covers 120 acres, and is occupied by vast and imposing prisons and asylums, built by the convicts from stone quarried on the island. At the south end is the Charity Hospital, with 1,200 beds and 24 skilful house-physicians. Next comes the great Penitentiary, where 1,200 unfortunate criminals are kept under guard. It has a battlemented roof and towers, and is built of granite and iron. More than half of the prisoners are foreigners. Farther north are the two great Almshouses, one for each sex, with high verandas and pleasant grounds. Farther up are the Workhouses, the City Lunatic-Asylum, and other cancer-spots of modern Manhattan. Visitors must get a pass at Third Avenue and 11th Street, and go over on the ferry from East 26th Street.

Governor's Island is a picturesque ornament of the inner harbor, about half a mile from the Battery, towards Brooklyn. It is the headquarters of the Military Department of the Atlantic (Major-Gen. Howard), and has forts galore, and parks of guns, magazines, barracks, and a beautiful parade-ground. At one end is the circular three-story stone fortress of Castle William, built in 1811, and at one time a prison for a thousand Southern soldiers; and near the centre are the low and massive walls of the star-shaped Fort Columbus. There are grand old trees on the island, the museum of the United Service Institution (including Gen. Sheridan's famous Winchester horse, mementos of Washington, Hogarth's painting implements, and *souvenirs* of Indian, East-Indian, and Secession wars), and the Chapel of Cornelius the Centurion. Steamboats run hourly from the Battery

COMMERCIAL BUILDINGS:

A FEW years ago, if a man wished to become a hermit, he would take an office on the fourth or fifth story of a building. No one would ascend to such dizzy heights, save an occasional daring book-agent or advertising solicitor, who, when he got there, would be too short of breath to explain his mission, or offer more than the feeblest opposition to his ejectment. The introduction of the passenger elevator has revolutionized this, and led to the construction of immensely lofty buildings for business purposes. Now the greater the altitude, the more desirable the accommodation. An office upon the tenth or twelfth story of one of these buildings is light, cool, airy, and quiet, and as easy of access as if nearer the ground.

Equitable Building on Broadway, between Cedar and Pine Streets, was finished in 1887, and is a mountainous pile of Quincy granite, solid and fireproof as a rock, and with four imposing façades, abounding in pillars and carvings. The high-arched Broadway entrance, 22 feet wide, leads to the finest court-yard in America, 100 by 44 feet in area, with a tessellated pavement, from which rise lines of rose-colored marble columns with onyx capitals, upholding an entablature of polished red granite, above which is a finely arched roof of stained glass and polished marble. The building fronts for 167½ feet on Broadway, and cost $8,000,000.

Mutual Life-Insurance Building is 165 feet high, fireproof, rich in marble, wrought-iron work, mahogany, Whittier elevators, and other modern architectural luxuries, and costing not far from $2,000,000.

Washington Building, on Broadway, Battery Place, and Greenwich Street, built by the great financier, Cyrus W. Field. It is twelve stories high, and the great observatory-tower reaches an altitude of 235 feet from the pavement. The top of the flag-staff is higher than Trinity spire or the Liberty statue. The view from the tower is the finest in the city, — one of the finest in the world.

Mills Building, on Broad Street, is a vast structure, forming three sides of a court-yard. It cost $2,700,000.

United Bank Building, at Broadway and Wall Street, the "Fort Sherman" of the financiers, contains the offices once occupied by Gen. Grant. Here Ferdinand Ward concocted his vast and historic swindles.

Standard Oil Company's Building, on Broadway, is the largest marble structure in New York. Here is the office of William Rockafeller.

Drexel Building, at Broad and Wall Streets, is of white marble, in Renaissance architecture, and cost $700,000.

Aldrich Court, on Broadway, opposite Exchange Place, is another lofty palace of trade. It was finished in 1887, and contains 300 offices, lighted at night by 2,600 Edison incandescent lights, and reached by four Otis elevators. It is built around a court-yard, 50 by 70 feet.

Manhattan Bank Building, on Wall Street, near Broad Street, is of polished gray granite, and is one of the finest structures in the city. It was finished in 1885, and is occupied by banks, lawyers, etc.

Trinity Building, on one of the Broadway sides of Trinity Church-yard, is a vast hive of lawyers, real-estate dealers, etc.

Boreel Building is an immense brick structure, filled with offices, largely of famous and powerful insurance companies.

Western Union Telegraph Building, at Dey Street and Broadway, is of brick, granite, and marble, eight stories high, with a tall tower.

Temple Court is a huge building 160 feet high, erected at a cost of $1,200,000, and belonging to Eugene Kelly. This is one of an amazing group of buildings at the corner of Nassau and Beekman Streets.

Potter Building, on the opposite corner, with fronts on Printing-house Square, Nassau and Beekman Streets, is of iron and brick, 185 feet high, and cost $2,500,000.

Morse Building, Nassau and Beekman Streets, ten stories (165 feet) high, is of red and black brick, and belongs to the son and nephew of Professor S. F. B. Morse. It is fireproof and massive.

Stewart Building, at Broadway and Chambers Street, of white marble, occupies the site of the ancient negro burying-ground, and afterward of Washington Hall. It was erected for A. T. Stewart.

HOSPITALS, DISPENSARIES, HOMES, Etc.

ALL over the city, there are hospitals and dispensaries, where the sick and ailing are treated and cared for. If the patient is poor, no charge is made: if able, he is expected to pay a moderate sum. The list is so great that we shall mention but a few, and then must refer the reader interested in such matters to the list in the City Directory. New York is peculiarly blessed in this most noble form of charity; and any one who is sick or ailing, however poor, will be cared for at one of these institutions. Even the dumb animals are provided for: there are two hospitals in the city where poor people may have their domestic animals doctored free, and where there are accommodations for sick horses and dogs.

In many of the hospitals, for $5,000 the donor and his successors have the privilege of nominating the occupant of a bed for all time. Frequently a bed is thus endowed in memory of some dead friend or relative, whose name it bears. Such a monument is more beautiful and enduring than any work of the sculptor's chisel.

There are also a great number of benevolent societies for the care of the blind, deaf and dumb, insane, aged, orphaned, indigent poor and friendless, of every sort and description. Many millions are annually spent on these charities.

Bloomingdale Asylum for the Insane, at Boulevard and 117th Street, on Washington Heights, is a palatial brown-stone building, erected mainly in 1821, amid charming grounds of 45 acres. Only paying patients are received.

Institution for the Deaf and Dumb, at Fanwood (162d Street), Washington Heights, is richly endowed, and has 37 acres of grounds. It was founded in 1816, and educates 250 pupils, the course being 8 years. Open daily, 1.30 to 4 P.M.

Institution for the Blind, at Ninth Avenue and West 34th Street, has a granite Gothic building. It was founded in 1831. Blind children are educated here, in letters and useful arts. Open to visitors, 1 to 6 P.M. daily.

New-York Hospital (15th Street, near Fifth Avenue) is a great, many-balconied, brick building, with ornamental Gothic gables. The institution was founded by the Earl of Dunmore, in 1771; and its ancient seat, between Duane and Church Streets and Broadway, was vacated in 1870, the present building being opened in 1877. Ward patients pay $1 a day.

St. Luke's Hospital, at Fifth Avenue and 54th Street, was founded in 1850 by the Rev. W. A. Muhlenberg, and has an oblong parallelogram of buildings, with wings, and a central chapel flanked with towers. It is attended by Episcopal nuns, and the form of worship is Episcopalian; but patients are received without regard to sect.

Orphan Asylum, at Riverside Park, was founded about 1807, in a small hired house below City-hall Park. Its property is now worth $1,000,000, and 200 orphans are in its charge.

Mount Sinai Hospital, at Lexington Avenue and East 66th Street, is a noble Elizabethan pile of brick and marble, admirably equipped, with nearly 200 free beds. It cost $340,000, and was erected by Jewish New-Yorkers, but is non-sectarian.

Presbyterian Hospital, at Madison Avenue and East 70th Street, founded by James Lenox, who also established the magnificent Lenox Library, is a handsome Gothic building, dating from 1872.

Cancer Hospital, The New York (there is but one other in the world), is on Eighth Avenue, near 105th Street. It was founded in 1884, with an endowment of $200,000 from John Jacob Astor, $50,000 from Mrs. Gen. Cullom, and $25,000 each from Mrs. Astor, Mrs. R. L. Stuart, and Mrs. C. H. Rogers.

Old Ladies' Home, of the Baptist Church, on 68th Street, near Fourth Avenue, is a spacious semi-Gothic building in the form of the letter H.

Roosevelt Hospital, at Ninth Avenue and 59th Street, richly endowed by the late James H. Roosevelt, is an admirably arranged and spacious pavilion hospital, opened in 1871, and accommodating 180 patients.

AMONG the other beneficent institutions of New York are,—

Actors' Fund, 12 West 28th Street.

American Dramatic-Fund, 1267 Broadway.

American Veterinary Hospital, 141 West 54th Street.

Artists' Fund Society, 6 Astor Place.

Association for Befriending Children and Young Girls, 136 Second Avenue. Catholic, for 200 vagrants.

Association for the Improved Instruction of Deaf-Mutes, Lexington Avenue and 67th Street.

Association for the Relief of Respectable Aged Indigent Females, Tenth Avenue and 104th Street. Founded 1814.

Asylum for Lying-in Women, 139 Second Avenue. Founded 1823.

Asylum of St. Vincent de Paul, 215 West 39th Street. For 150 orphans.

Baptist Home for Aged Persons, Fourth Avenue and 68th Street.

Bethany Institute for Woman's Christian Work, 69 Second Avenue.

Bible and Fruit Mission, East 26th Street.

Bread and Beef House, 139 West 48th Street.

Catholic Protectory, at Fordham.

Chambers-Street Hospital, 160 Chambers Street.

Chapin Home for the Aged and Infirm, 151 East 66th Street.

Charity Organization Society, 21 University Place.

Children's Aid Society, 24 St. Mark's Place.

City Mission Society, 306 Mulberry Street.

Colored Home and Hospital, First Avenue and 65th Street.

Colored Orphan Asylum, Tenth Avenue and 143d Street. 300 beneficiaries. Founded 1837.

Day Nursery and Babies' Shelter, 118 West 21st Street.

Emergency Hospital, 223 East 26th Street.

Female Assistance Society, 288 Madison Avenue.

Five-Points House of Industry, 155 Worth Street.

Five-Points Mission, 61 Park Street.

Foundling Asylum, 68th Street, near Third Avenue.

Free Home for Destitute Young Girls, 23 East 11th Street.

Friends' Employment Society, Rutherford Place.

Grace Memorial House, 94 Fourth Avenue.

Hahnemann Homœopathic Hospital, Fourth Avenue, near East 67th Street.

Harlem Hospital, 27 West 124th Street.

Hebrew Benevolent and Orphan Asylum Society, Tenth Avenue and West 136th Street.

Home for Aged Hebrews, 105th Street, near Tenth Avenue.

Home for Aged Men and Women, 106th Street, near Ninth Avenue.

Home for Colored Aged, foot of East 65th Street.

Home for Convalescent, 433 East 118th Street.

Home for Deaf-Mutes, 220 East 13th Street.

Home for Fallen and Friendless Girls, 49 West 4th Street.

Home for Incurables, Fordham Avenue and East 182d Street.

Home for Inebriates, Madison Avenue and 86th Street.

Home for Mothers and Infants, Tenth Avenue and West 61st Street.

Home for Old Men and Aged Couples, 487 Hudson Street.

Home for Sailors, 190 Cherry Street.

Home for the Aged Poor, 231 West 38th Street, and 179 East 70th Street.

Home for the Friendless, 32 East 30th Street.

Home for Women, 273 Water Street, 260 Greene Street.

Home of Industry for Reformed Men, 40 East Houston Street.

Hospital New-York College of Veterinary Surgeons, East 58th Street, near Fifth Avenue.

Hospital for Ruptured and Crippled, Lexington Avenue and 42d Street.

House of Industry, 120 West 16th Street, for females only.

House of Mercy, West 86th Street.

House of Rest for Consumptives, at Fordham.

House of the Good Shepherd, East 89th Street.

Howard Mission, 40 New Bowery.

Infant Asylum, Tenth Avenue and East 61st Street.

Institution for the Blind, Ninth Avenue and 34th Street.

Institution for the Deaf and Dumb, Tenth Avenue and 162d Street.
Institution of Mercy, 33 East Houston Street.
Juvenile Asylum, Tenth Avenue and 176th Street.
Ladies' Helping Hand Association, 160 West 29th Street.
Leake and Watts Orphan House, Ninth Avenue and 111th Street.
Magdalen Asylum, 88th Street, near Fifth Avenue.
Manhattan Eye and Ear Hospital, 103 Park Avenue.
Masonic Board of Relief, Masonic Temple.
Medical Mission, 81 Roosevelt Street.
Methodist-Episcopal Home, West 92d Street and Tenth Avenue.
For aged and infirm.
Metropolitan Throat Hospital, 351 West 34th Street.
Midnight Mission, 260 Greene Street.   For fallen women.
New-York Eye and Ear Infirmary, Second Avenue and 13th Street.
New-York Infirmary for Women and Children, 5 Livingston Place.
New-York Ophthalmic Hospital, 201 East 23d Street.
Nursery and Child's Hospital, Lexington Avenue and 51st Street.
Olivet Helping Hand, 63 2d Street.
Orphan Asylum (Catholic), Fifth Avenue and Madison Avenue,
between 51st and 52d Streets.   1,200 children.
Orphan's Home (Episcopal), 49th Street, near Lexington Avenue.
Peabody Home for Aged Women, West Farms.
Presbyterian Home for Aged Women, 73d Street, near Madison
Avenue.
St. Barnabas Home, 304 Mulberry Street.
St. Elizabeth Hospital, 225 West 31st Street.
St. Francis Hospital, 605 5th Street.
St. John's Guild, 8 University Place.
St. Joseph's Orphan Asylum, Avenue A and 89th Street.
State Charities Aid Association, 21 University Place.
Trinity Hospital, 50 Varick Street.
Women's Christian Temperance Home, 440 East 57th Street.
Women's Hospital, Fourth Avenue and 49th Street.
Young Women's Home, 27 Washington Square.

A STROLL UP FIFTH AVENUE.

FIFTH AVENUE is the Belgravia of the American metropolis the centre of its fashion and splendor, the home of its merchant princes. It is at its best on a pleasant Sunday, at the time when the churches are out; or on a bright afternoon, when its long lines of carriages are rumbling away towards the Park. The scene of beauty and animation then presented is unequalled in America (or in Europe or Asia, for that matter); and in the perfect costumes of the promenaders, the dignity of the equipages, the variety and beauty of the domestic and ecclesiastical architecture, affords numberless objects of interest for the amazed and delighted provincial philosopher.

Here, on every side, are gorgeous club-houses, churches notable for their beauty, and a domestic architecture of rare variety and comfort, with picture-galleries, and rich porticos, and long vistas of Connecticut brown-stone palaces, the homes of incalculable wealth and splendor. From its beginning in Washington Square, the avenue traverses miles of a palatial residence-quarter, until it reaches Central Park, and passes on, a league beyond, into the suburban life of Harlem.

In taking a stroll up Fifth Avenue, of about a league, one should be accompanied by a herald king-at-arms, a mercantile register, an *élite* directory, and a wise old club-man with his stores of personal and family gossip. In default of these, we have strung together here a few items of interest, which may interest the passing tourist.

The blue omnibuses of the Fifth-avenue Transportation Company, limited, run at frequent intervals from Bleecker Street up South Fifth Avenue, across Washington Square, and along the avenue to 89th Street (fare, 5 cents).

Washington Square, where Fifth Avenue begins, is a park of nine acres, occupying the mournful site of the old Potter's Field, wherein more than 100,000 human bodies were buried. On its east side is the white-stone Gothic building of the University of the City of New York, with 800 students and 64 instructors. It is described by Theodore Winthrop in his brilliant novel of " Cecil Dreeme." On and near the square dwell Charles DeKay, the poet; the famous saltatory Kiralfy family; Augustus St. Gaudens, the sculptor; the De Navarro fami-lies, Walter Shirlaw; Gaston L. Feuardent, the antiquary; and other notable persons.

At No. 1, the first house on the right, as the avenue leaves Wash-ington Square, lives William Butler Duncan; and on the other side, at 6 and 8, are the Lispenard Stewarts, and John Taylor Johnston, the famous art-connoisseur. Beyond Clinton Place is the aristocratic Brevoort House, a favorite with English tourists and me-luds; and opposite is the Berkeley. where Theodore Thomas and many others dwell. Beyond 9th Street, at No. 23, lives Gen. Daniel E. Sickles. At 10th Street is the brown-stone Church of the Ascension (Episco-pal), with the Grosvenor opposite. The First Presbyterian Church comes next, with the Minturn and Talbot mansions beyond. At 14th Street we see the busy precincts of Union Square, to the right, and traverse a region of brilliant shops. On the left-hand corner of 15th Street is the great and finely appointed brown-stone building of the Manhattan Club,* the favorite resort of the patricians of the Demo-cratic party, called by their round-headed fellow-partisans " the swal-low-tails." It has 1,000 members ; and the entrance fee is $100, with $70 yearly dues. Across Union Square, 109 East 15th Street, is the house of the famous Century Association, a literary, artistic, and æs-thetic club, with 600 members, a large library, and a picture-gallery.

On West 15th Street are the spacious buildings of the College of St. Francis Xavier, with nearly 500 students, and a library of 20,000 volumes. On West 16th Street is the tall New-York Hospital, char-tered by King George III. in 1771.

At the farther right corner of 16th Street formerly lived Levi P. Morton (No. 85), and Col. Robert G. Ingersoll lives at No. 89. At No. 103 is the home of Edwards Pierrepont, long time Minister to England. At No. 118 live the New-York Winthrops. At 18th Street

---

* Recently moved to the Stewart house, corner 34th Street.

is the rich and ornate Chickering Hall, devoted to musical entertain
ments; and opposite, at No. 109, is August Belmont's estate, where
also dwells the Hon. Perry Belmont, a well-known Congressman. On
the opposite corner, at No. 107, is the mansion of Mrs. Marshall O.
Roberts, one of the grand dames of New-York society. On the 21st-
street corner is the great brown-stone building of the patrician Union
Club, founded in 1836, and with over 1,000 members. The entrance-
fee is $300, and yearly dues $75. Clarence A. Seward, the gifted son
of William H. Seward, lives at No. 143. At No. 147 (corner of East
21st Street) is the Lotos Club's comfortable brown-stone building,
with 500 members, where famous monthly art-receptions and ladies'
days are held. Here dwells the veteran world-traveller, Col. Thomas
W. Knox. Next door is the Glenham Hotel. In this vicinity stands
the South Reformed Church (corner of West 21st Street), and the
Cumberland is between East 22d and East 23d Streets. Now the
avenue cuts obliquely across Broadway, with the brilliant vistas of
Madison Square on the right, passing the enormous white-marble
Fifth-avenue Hotel, the home of Gen. W. T. Sherman, Ex-Senator
Platt, William J. Florence, and other notable persons. On the next
block is the Hoffman House, famous for its interior decorations and
magnificent bar-room. At 25th Street is the old home of the fashionable New-York Club. At the corner of West 26th Street is Delmon-
ico's famous restaurant, with Hotel Brunswick opposite.

At West 27th Street is the immense and lofty Victoria Hotel,
towering high above the surrounding buildings. At Fifth Avenue
and 28th Street (No. 247) was the home of the late Professor E. L.
Youmans, editor of the " Popular Science Monthly," and author of
many famous scientific books. No. 244 is the home of the famous
Mrs. Paran Stevens, and at No. 9 West 29th Street lived Ex-Senator
Roscoe Conkling, one of the great legal luminaries and orators of
New York.

On the next block is the great and costly Knickerbocker. The
great double house, No. 259, is Mrs. Josephine May's, and belonged
to her father, the late George Law, millionnaire and financier. At No.
26 (corner of East 29th Street) dwells Gen. George W. Cullom,

beyond the Hamersley mansions. At West 29th Street appears the white granite temple of the Fifth-avenue Reformed Church; and a little way to the right (on 29th Street) is the picturesque Church of the Transfiguration (Episcopal), generally and affectionately known as "The Little Church around the Corner," wherefrom many actors have been buried. The bit of green lawn, overarching trees, and mantling of ivy, make this a charming oasis in the surrounding desert of brick and stone. The corner of 30th Street is marked by the new and attractive hotel, " Holland House."

The towering Gilsey House rises to the left, on West 30th Street. At No. 319 (corner of East 32d Street) stands the new house of the exclusive Knickerbocker Club, which includes many well-known devotees of coaching and polo. Its entrance-fee is $300, annual dues $100. Between West 32d and West 33d Streets (Nos. 338 and 350), once huge brick mansions of the hundred-millionnaire brothers,— John Jacob Astor and William Astor,—a superb hotel is being erected. On the next corner, at No. 374, is the town-house of Mrs. J. Coleman Drayton, one of the Astor daughters. At the corner of West 34th Street is the great Italian palace of white marble, erected at a cost of $2,000,000 by the late A. T. Stewart, a Belfast lad, who came to America in 1818, and began life in New York as an assistant teacher, then opened a small shop for trimmings, and in time became the most successful merchant in the world, so that when he died (in 1876), he left $40,000,000. Mrs. Stewart lived here until her death, in 1886.* Alongside the Stewart place, the only other house on the block, is the great old Astor mansion, which, after a strangely checkered career, has just been leased by the New-York Club, to be dedicated to their joyous uses.

Between West 35th Street and West 36th Streets live the Kernochans (No. 384), and Gen. Daniel Butterfield (No. 386); and at No. 389 (between East 36th and 37th Streets) is Pierre Lorillard's home. The fashionable Christ Church (Episcopal), famous for its fine music and beautiful frescos, is on the corner of West 35th Street; and the Brick Church (Presbyterian) rises at the corner of

* It is now the home of the Manhattan Club.

West 37th Street. At the old home of Gov. E. D. Morgan, No. 415 (between East 37th and 38th Streets), is the St. Nicholas Club, composed exclusively of gentlemen of the oldest Knickerbocker families, — the Remsens, De Peysters, Rhinelanders, Roosevelts, etc. At No. 425 (beyond East 38th Street) is the home of Austin Corbin, the railway king ; at No. 429 that of the late Henry Bergh, the friend of suffering animals ; at No. 459 (beyond East 39th Street) that of Frederick W. Vanderbilt.

The lofty and quaint Union League Club-house is at the corner of Fifth Avenue and East 39th Street, with its conspicuous gables and huge roof. From West 40th to 42d Street extends the Distributing Reservoir of the Croton Water-Works, crowning the summit of Murray Hill, 115 feet above tide-water, covering 4 acres, and holding 23,000,000 gallons of water. It is a massive structure in Egyptian architecture, 44 feet high, and 420 feet square. Back of it is the pleasant Bryant Park, on which the famous Crystal Palace stood, thirty years or more ago.   Opposite, on Fifth Avenue, are the tall art-furniture buildings of Ball, Graves and others, the massive American Safe-Deposit building, and a few quaint dwellings, the remnants of the old-time block of yellow Gothic houses (one of them still occupied by Mrs. Lucian B. Chase), in part of which was the famous Rutgers Female College. Next the avenue crosses 42d Street, which runs to the left to the Weehawken Ferry, and to the right to the Grand Central Depot, and the Grand Union Hotel, our comfortable headquarters in New York.

On the left corner of Fifth Avenue and 42d Street is the lofty stone Hotel Bristol, with Russell Sage's house next door (No. 406), and opposite is the Hamilton. At the corner of East 43d Street is the Temple Emanu-El, the great Hebrew synagogue, perhaps the richest piece of Saracenic architecture in America, with its minaret-like towers, delicate carvings, Oriental arches, and a dazzlingly brilliant interior. In the next block is the Sherwood, the home of Jesse Seligman, the banker, the Rev. G. H. Hepworth, and other well-known persons. Opposite, at 524, were headquarters of the Manhattan Athletic Club, with its luxurious rooms, and finely equipped gymnasium. At No.

532 is Manton Marble's house, and No. 549 is Thomas T. Eckert's home. The Universalist Church of the Divine Paternity, so long ministered to by Dr. Chapin, stands at the corner of West 45th Street. A little way to the right, on East 45th Street, are the homes of the famous broker, Washington E. Conner (No. 14), and of the eloquent Chauncy M. Depew, president of the New-York Central Railroad (No. 22), and one of the best after-dinner speakers in America. At No. 2 East 46th Street is the mansion of Seligman, the well-known financier. Nearly opposite the Universalist Church is the narrow and richly carved façade of the Episcopal Church of the Heavenly Rest, whose interior is rich in polished granite pillars, with quaintly carved capitals, frescos after Fra Angelico, and other beautiful adornments. The great Windsor Hotel extends from East 46th to East 47th Street, and is the home of Andrew Carnegie, and many other noted men. Opposite, at No. 562, dwells Joseph W. Harper, jun., of the famous publishing-house; and at No. 574 are the rooms of the American Yacht Club, famous for its navy of costly steam-yachts. On the corner beyond the Windsor, at No. 579, in a large brown-stone house, with lanterns in front, lives Jay Gould, the Napoleon of finance; and at the other end of the block, with carved stone griffins in front, is the home of Robert Goelet. The Goelet estate is above $20,000,000. At No. 50 West 47th Street lives Joseph H. Choate, lawyer and orator, and one of the greatest after-dinner speakers of this age. At West 48th Street is the ornate and high-spired Collegiate Dutch Church, with its flying buttresses, carved portals, and general richness of detail; and the second house beyond (No. 608) pertains to Ogden Goelet. At the corner of East 48th Street (No. 597) is the home of Roswell P. Flower, eminent in latter-day politics. The next block, from East 49th to 50th Street, is taken up largely by the great Buckingham Hotel, a quiet and expensive family hotel; and at No. 615 lives Edward S. Jaffray, the dry-goods merchant. Opposite, at No. 624, is the house of the late John Roach, the great ship-builder.

At the corner of 50th Street rises the vast Cathedral of St. Patrick, described in the chapter on Churches.

At No. 634, opposite the Cathedral, is the home of D. O. Mills, ex-senator from California, and father-in-law of Whitelaw Reid, of the "Tribune." Back of the Cathedral is the Florentine palace built by Henry Villard, alongside of Columbia College. Beyond the Cathedral, on Fifth Avenue, is the Roman-Catholic Orphan Asylum for Boys, on high ground, with the Asylum for Orphan Girls behind it. Between West 51st and 52d Streets are the magnificent brown-stone palaces of the Vanderbilt family, enriched by broad bands of carved foliage, and superbly furnished and decorated inside. No. 640 is the home of Mrs. William H. Vanderbilt, and No. 642 is the home of her daughter, Mrs. William D. Sloane.

Across West 52d Street rises the handsome white-stone French *château* of William K. Vanderbilt, rich in carvings and oriel-windows. The author of "Recent Architecture in America" calls this "the most beautiful house in New York."

Next comes the beautiful and fashionable Episcopal Church of St. Thomas, famous for society weddings. It is a brown-stone Gothic structure, with a melodious chime of bells, and famous altar-paintings by LaFarge. Among its clergy have been Bishops Upfold and Whitehouse, and the Rev. Dr. F. L. Hawks. Just beyond, on the same square, are the picturesque connected mansions of Dr. W. S. Webb and Hamilton McK. Twombly, who married daughters of William H. Vanderbilt. Between East 52d and 53d Streets is the Langham. Between West 54th and 55th Streets are the spacious buildings and grounds of St. Luke's Hospital (open to visitors from 10 to 12, Tuesdays, Thursdays, and Saturdays), where Episcopal Sisters of the Holy Communion attend the sick, without regard to their sect or nation.

In this vicinity dwell several of the Standard-Oil Company magnates, — Henry M. Flagler at No. 685, William Rockefeller at No. 689, etc.

At West 55th Street is the great Presbyterian Church under Dr. John Hall's ministration, the largest church of that sect in the world, with a spire that is a landmark for a great distance. No. 724, just beyond West 56th Street, is the home of R. Fulton Cutting, — a very handsome piece of domestic architecture. At the lower corner of

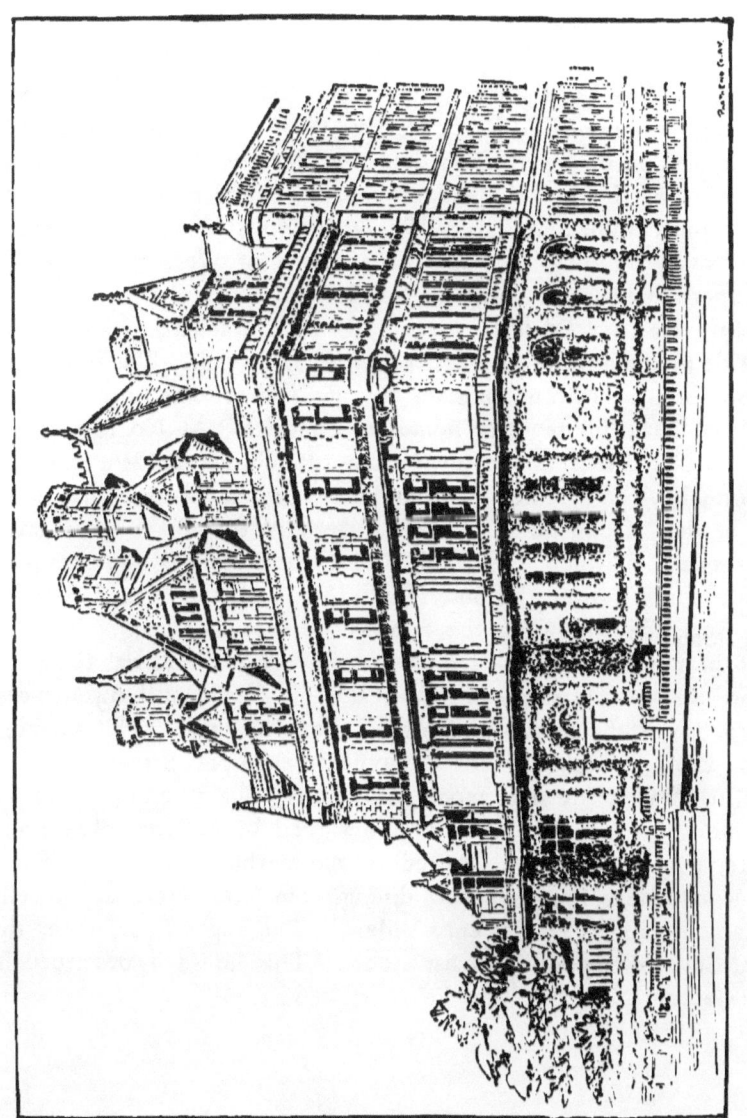

RESIDENCE OF CORNELIUS VANDERBILT.

West 57th Street is the handsome house built and some time occupied by the famous Mrs. Frederick W. Stevens, the immensely wealthy heiress of Josiah Sampson, who deserted her husband after twenty years of married life, and in 1886 married the Marquis de Talleyrand-Perigord, in Paris. The house now belongs to Secretary-of-the-Navy Whitney. On the other corner of West 57th Street is the superb mansion of Cornelius Vanderbilt.

A little way beyond is the beginning of Central Park, which forms one side of the avenue for over two miles and a half. The other side is being built up with noble mansions, and will at some future time be the most beautiful place of homes in America. At No. 810, corner of East 62d Street, is the town-house of William Belden, a many millionnaire, who defeated Jay Gould in the famous Black-Friday financial battle. Opposite East 64th Street is the old Arsenal and Menagerie. Between East 66th and 67th Streets is the group of houses in which dwell the Soto family (No. 854), and Mrs. de Barrios (No. 855), the widow of the famous Central-American statesman, killed in battle a few years ago. No. 3 East 66th Street was the home of the late Gen. Ulysses S. Grant, and his family still dwell there. At No. 871 is the mansion of Mrs. Robert L. Stuart. The splendid Lenox Library extends from East 70th Street to 71st Street.

A little way to the right looms up the lofty, quaint, and picturesque gray house of Charles L. Tiffany, designed by McKim, Mead, and White, with its mediæval portcullis, red-marble Moorish stairway, teak-wood doors, blue-and-pearl dining-room, etc. Here also dwells the famous railway king, Henry Villard. The upper floor, under the great, dusky tiled roof, is a vast studio. This house is described in the "Century Magazine" for February, 1886.

A HUDSON-RIVER STEAMER.

NEW YORK IN SUMMER.

EXCURSIONS AND ISLAND RESORTS.

Hot nights in New York are rare.   At dusk, on the warmest days of summer, a sea-breeze springs up, which makes the nights cool and delightful.   No other city offers such an endless variety of excursions on river, harbor, bay, and ocean.   Completely surrounded by water, at the mouth of the magnificent Hudson, and hard by the broad Atlantic, New York offers countless attractions to those in search of rest, recreation, and health.   Every day, for weeks, some new excursion on the water may be taken, leaving the city in the morning, and returning in the cool of the evening.   The city hotels are not full in summer; and travellers can be made more comfortable than in crowded seaside resorts, and at much less cost.

Space will permit us to mention only a few of the excursions.

The Hudson River. — First and foremost among the pleasure excursions is a trip on the Hudson.   The swift and splendid steamers of the Hudson-river Day Line leave the foot of West 22d Street every morning except Sunday during the season at 9 o'clock, arriving at Albany at 6.10 P.M.   The best way to reach the pier from the Grand Union Hotel, is to take the Fourth-avenue cars, which pass the door, to 23d Street, and the 23d-street cars across to the North River.   On leaving the pier, a fine view of New-York City and harbor is obtained; while on the opposite shore are Jersey City and Hoboken, and Weehawken, where Alexander Hamilton was killed in a duel with Aaron Burr.   On the east bank may soon be seen the tomb of Gen. Grant.   At Fort Washington and Fort Lee (ten miles up) begins the historic part of the river, for a description of which we must refer the reader to some more assuming work.   "The Hudson by Daylight," an excellent descriptive guide of the river, for sale on the boats, is recommended.   The " Panoramic View of the Hudson " is also worth purchasing

The Palisades on the west bank begin here, and extend up the river for fifteen or twenty miles. They are bare, precipitous walls of rock, which rise abruptly from the river to a height of 250 to 600 feet. Passing Yonkers on the right, we see "Greystone," the residence of the late Samuel J. Tilden. From here to and beyond Tarrytown, the east bank is lined with palatial residences. At *Irvington*, on the right, we catch a glimpse of Sunnyside, where Washington Irving lived. On the west bank, a few miles above, is *Tappan*, where André was executed. On the east bank is *Lyndehurst*, the summer home of Jay Gould; and *Tarrytown*, where Major André was captured. A mile above Tarrytown is the Old Dutch Church, where Washington Irving is buried. At *Sing Sing*, on the east bank, thirty-two miles from New York, the State Prison is located. Soon the river broadens into a bay five miles wide, at the northern end of which, on the west bank, is *Stony Point*, sometimes known as "Mad Anthony's Charge." Here Gen. Anthony Wayne, in the dead of night, with a handful of men, surprised and recaptured the British fort on Stony Point. Readers of Thackeray's "Virginians" will remember his thrilling account of this battle. The river here is only half a mile wide. On the east bank is *Verplanck's Point*, the site of Fort Lafayette, where Baron Steuben drilled soldiers for the Revolutionary army. At this point the river appears to end. On the west bank rises the *Dunderberg* mountain, made famous by Irving; and on the east *Anthony's Nose*, over 1,200 feet high; and between the two, and apparently completely shutting in the river, lies *Iona Island*, a popular excursion resort. Rounding this island, we come into full view of the historic Highlands of the Hudson. On the west bank lies *West Point*, where visitors may land, and visit the Military Academy, fort, and historic spots. Three delightful hours may be spent here, when the down-boat from *Albany* may be taken, reaching New York at 6 P.M. If visitors prefer, they may keep on up the river, passing on the east bank *Garrison's* and *Storm King*, the highest peak of the Highlands, to *Newburg*, where they may visit Washington's headquarters, and stand upon the spot where he read his farewell address to the American army. One hour and a half may be spent here, before the arrival of the down-boat.

There are excellent restaurants on the steamers, on the European plan. Strangers visiting New York should not miss this trip, which is a most beautiful and interesting one.

Coney Island, five miles in length, is about ten miles from the New York City Hall, and is bounded on the south by the Atlantic Ocean. It is divided into four parts, known as *Norton's Point* (which is little frequented), *West Brighton, Brighton*, and *Manhattan Beach.* There are various rail and steamboat routes to the island (see daily papers); but perhaps the pleasantest way of getting there, is to take one of the Iron Steamboat Company's vessels from the foot of West 23d Street, or Pier 1, North River. They leave hourly during the season, and land at the Iron Pier, West Brighton. Excursion tickets, 50 cents. Another good route is to take steamer from foot of Whitehall Street (South-ferry Station, Third-avenue line) to Bay Ridge, and, from there, train to West Brighton or Manhattan Beach. Excursion tickets 50 cents.

Norton's Point, or West End, is the secluded portion of Coney Island, and a visit is not recommended.

West Brighton is the democratic part of the island. It is made up of a motley collection of hotels, large and small, concert stands, beer-gardens, variety-shows, skating-rinks, wooden toboggan-slides, shooting-galleries, bathing-houses, merry-go-rounds, inclined-railways, museums, aquariums, brass-bands, pop-corn and hot sausage venders; in fact, it is like a great country-fair in full blast, crowded with every-day people, out for a good time. Here is an iron observatory 300 feet high, with elevators running to the top; a camera-obscura; two iron piers upwards of a thousand feet long, with bathing-houses beneath; and a building in the shape of a colossal elephant, with restaurants, dancing-rooms, and various exhibitions inside, and an observatory on top. The pell-mell excitement of the place is kept up all day and until almost midnight throughout the week, with no cessation on Sunday. Half a mile east along the beach is Brighton. Stages run this distance (fare 5 cents), and there is also an elevated road.

Brighton Beach. — Here there is an enormous hotel, capable of dining 20,000 people in a day. The grounds are handsomely laid out and ornamented with flowers, and the bathing facilities are excellent. In a pavilion a large orchestra gives concerts afternoon and evening. East of Brighton Beach, for 2½ miles, extend the grounds of

Manhattan Beach. — (Reached by a small railway, fare 5 cents.) This is the best part of the island, and is patronized by the better classes. The hotel is nearly 700 feet long, and is one of the largest structures of its kind in the world. 4,000 people can dine at a time, and 30,000 during the day. The grounds are beautifully laid out, and there are concerts afternoon and evening in a pavilion in front of the hotel. There are 2,700 rooms in the bathing establishment, and an amphitheatre for spectators to watch the bathers, in which a band plays afternoon and evening. Bathing is perfectly safe.

East of the Manhattan Hotel comes the Oriental Hotel, a large and costly house for permanent guests. Manhattan Beach can be reached by rail direct from Long-Island City (East 34th-street Ferry), or by boat, from South Ferry to Bay Ridge, and thence by train. Several times a week, during the summer, wonderful displays of fire-works take place at the Brighton and Manhattan hotels, those of the latter place being unequalled elsewhere in the country. The Coney-Island Jockey-Club has a club-house at Manhattan Beach, and a fine race-track at Sheepshead Bay (just back of the beach), where race-meetings are held in June and September.

Rockaway Beach, on the Long-Island shore, is twenty miles from New York. It may be reached by rail (ferry from foot East 34th Street to Southern Railroad, Long Island); but the better way is to go by one of the immense excursion steamers, which run every few hours during the season. For time and place of sailing, see daily papers. This trip is strongly recommended. The sail is a fine one, affording splendid views of the harbor, shipping, and fortifications, and a sail on the Atlantic. The beach has most of the characteristics of Coney Island, but the surf is finer. The sail occupies an hour and a half each way. Excursion tickets, 50 cents. On Sunday the boats are often uncomfortably crowded.

Long Branch is on the New-Jersey coast, about thirty miles from New York. It is so well known that no description is necessary here. Steamers run, during the season, from Pier 8, North River, to Sandy Hook, and thence by rail to the Branch. This is the best route. It is also reached by the New-Jersey Southern and Pennsylvania Railroads. During the season, there are excursion steamers, which go all the way by water, landing passengers at the Long-Branch Iron Pier. (See daily papers.) The latter route is not recommended, as rough weather often prevents a landing.

Long Beach is on the Long-Island coast, east of Rockaway. There is but one hotel there, — an immense one, — and a number of cottages. The bathing facilities are perfect, and the surf usually runs high. A fine orchestra plays in front of the hotel morning and evening. A visit is strongly recommended to those who desire to spend a quiet and restful day by the sea, away from the "madding crowd." It is reached *via* Long-Island Railroad, ferry foot East 34th Street. Excursion tickets, 50 cents.

Glen Island, in Long-Island Sound, near New Rochelle, is a beautiful and picturesque summer resort for excursionists, with facilities for boating, bathing, sailing, fish-dinners, etc. The sail up the East River, past the various public institutions, and the Navy Yard, through Hell Gate, and out into the Sound, is an interesting one. Boats leave several times a day. See daily papers. Excursion tickets, 40 cents.

Staten Island, thirteen miles long, is in New-York Harbor. Boats run from South Ferry every half-hour. It is a hilly and picturesque island, dotted with fine houses and villas. On the eastern shore is Fort Wadsworth and Battery Hudson. On the north shore is the Sailors' Snug Harbor, an asylum for aged and infirm sailors, capable of accommodating over 1,000 persons. Of late the island has become a great centre for the amusement-loving public. A company has been organized, which, during the warm season, gives open-air entertainments on a colossal scale, which are attended daily and nightly by thousands. The fare is ten cents.

ELEVATED RAILWAYS.

Second Avenue Line.—(Daily, including Sundays.)

ROUTE.—Commencing at South Ferry, through Whitehall Street to Front Street, to Coenties Slip, to Pearl Street, to New Bowery, to Chatham Square, through Division Street to Allen Street, to First Avenue, to 23d Street, to 2d Avenue, to 129th Street. Total distance, 8.73 miles. Heaviest grade, 73 feet per mile. This line is open from 5.30 A.M. to 11.58 P.M., including Sundays. Last train from 129th Street, South Bound, 11.58 P.M. Last train from South Ferry, North Bound, 12.46 A.M. Passengers for 34th Street Ferry, East River, change cars at 34th Street Station and take branch train for ferry. No extra charge. Passengers to or from City Hall change cars and cross the Bridge at Chatham Square Station. Passengers to or from Suburban Rapid Transit Railway change cars at 129th Street.

STATIONS.

NAME.	LOCATION.	NUMBERS AT INTERSECTION.
South Ferry.	Foot Whitehall St.	66 Whitehall—1 South St.
Hanover Square.	Pearl and S. William Sts.	110 Pearl—1 South William St.
Fulton St.*	Pearl and Fulton Sts.	266 Pearl—38 Fulton St.
Franklin Square.	Pearl and Cherry Sts.	340 Pearl—12 Cherry St.
Chatham Square.	Chatham Sq. and Bowery.	Chatham Sq.—1 Bowery.
Canal St.*	Allen and Canal Sts.	14 Allen—71 Canal St.
Grand St.*	Allen and Grand Sts.	66 Allen—309 Grand St.
Rivington St.	Allen and Rivington Sts.	140 Allen—70 Rivington St.
First St.	First St. and 1st Ave.	11 1st Ave.—73 First St.
Eighth St.*	Eighth St. and 1st Ave.	132 1st Ave.—87 Eighth St.
Fourteenth St.*	14th St. and 1st Ave.	240 1st Ave.—350 E. 14th St.
Nineteenth St.	19th St. and 1st Ave.	330 1st Ave.—358 E. 19th St.
Twenty-third St.*	23d St., bet. 1st and 2d Avs.	300 E. 23d St.—248 2d Ave.
Thirty-fourth St.*	34th St. and 2d Ave.	620 2d Ave.—300 E. 34th St.
Forty-second St.*	42d St. and 2d Ave.	782 2d Ave.—236 E. 42d St.
Fiftieth St.	50th St. and 2d Ave.	950 2d Ave.—253 E. 50th St.
Fifty-seventh St.	57th St. and 2d Ave.	1080 2d Ave.—250 E. 57th St.

* Crosstown car lines.

STATIONS.—*Continued.*

NAME.	LOCATION.	NUMBERS AT INTERSECTION.
Sixty-fifth St.	65th St. and 2d Ave.	1240 2d Ave.—252 E. 65th St.
Seventieth St.	70th St. and 2d Ave.	1330 2d Ave.—234 E. 70th St.
Seventy-fifth St.	75th St. and 2d Ave.	1440 2d Ave.—252 E. 75th St.
Eightieth St.	80th St. and 2d Ave.	1538 2d Ave.—248 E. 80th St.
Eighty-sixth St.	86th St. and 2d Ave.	1657 2d Ave.—242 E. 86th St.
Ninety-second St.	92d St. and 2d Ave.	1780 2d Ave.—300 E. 92d St.
Ninety-ninth Street.	99th St. and 2d Ave.	1913 2d Ave.—... E. 99th St.
111th Street.	111th St. and 2d Ave.	2160 2d Ave.—248 E. 111th St.
117th Street.	117th St. and 2d Ave.	2276 2d Ave.—252 E. 117th St.
121st Street.	121st St. and 2d Ave.	2358 2d Ave.—250 E. 121st St.
127th Street.	127th St. and 2d Ave.	2479 2d Ave.—245 E. 127th St.
129th Street.	129th St. and 2d Ave.	............—252 E. 129th St.

Third Avenue Line.—(Daily, including Sundays.)

ROUTE.—Commencing at South Ferry, through Whitehall Street to Front Street, to Coenties Slip, to Pearl Street, to New Bowery, to Chatham Square, to Bowery, to 3d Avenue, to 129th Street. 34th Street Branch ; from 3d Avenue, through 34th Street, to Ferry on East River. 42d Street Branch ; from 3d Avenue, through 42d Street, to Grand Central Depot, 42d Street and 4th Avenue. City Hall Branch ; from City Hall, through Chatham Street, to Chatham Square. Total distance, Main Line, 8.48 miles. Length of 34th Street Branch, 0.31 miles. Length of 42d Street Branch, 0.18 miles. Length of City Hall Branch, 0.36 miles. Heaviest grade on main line, 105 feet per mile. This line, including City Hall Branch, is open at all hours of the day and night, including Sundays. City Hall passengers to or from 2d Avenue Line change cars and cross the Bridge at Chatham Square Station. Direct connection made at City Hall Station, without going to the street, with trains crossing Brooklyn Bridge. Passengers for Grand Central Depot change cars at 42d Street Station and take branch train, which is run from 6.00 A.M. to 12.00 midnight. No extra charge. Passengers for 34th Street Ferry, East River, change cars at 34th Street Station and take branch train, which is run from 5.30 A.M. to 12.00 midnight. No extra charge.

STATIONS.

NAME.	LOCATION.	NUMBERS AT INTERSECTION.
South Ferry.	Foot Whitehall St.	66 Whitehall—1 South St.
Hanover Square.	Pearl and S. William Sts.	110 Pearl—1 South William St.
Fulton St.*	Pearl and Fulton Sts.	266 Pearl St.—38 Fulton St.
Franklin Square.	Pearl and Cherry Sts.	340 Pearl—12 Cherry St.
City Hall.	Chatham and Centre Sts.	N. Y. Terminus B'klyn Bridge.
Chatham Square.	Chatham Sq. and Bowery.	Chatham Sq.— 1 Bowery.
Canal St.*	Bowery and Canal St.	60 Bowery—150 Canal St.
Grand St.*	Bowery and Grand St.	122 Bowery—235 Grand St.
Houston St.*	Bowery and Houston St.	280 Bowery—90 E. Houston St.
Ninth St.*	3d Ave. and 9th St.	31 3d Ave.—117 E. 9th St.
Fourteenth St.*	3d Ave. and 14th St.	123 3d Ave.—152 E. 14th St.
Eighteenth St.*	3d Ave. and 18th St.	205 3d Ave.—148 E. 18th St.
Twenty-third St.*	3d Ave. and 23d St.	300 3d Ave.—164 E. 23d St.
Twenty-eighth St.	3d Ave. and 28th St.	392 3d Ave.—161 E. 28th St.
Thirty-fourth St.*	3d Ave. and 34th St.	507 3d Ave.—166 E. 34th St.
34th Street Ferry.	Foot 34th St., E. R.	408 E. 34th St.
Forty-second St.*	3d Ave. and 42d St.	657 3d Ave.—164 E. 42d St.
Grand Central.*	42d St. and 4th Ave.	Grand Central Depot.
Forty-seventh St.	3d Ave. and 47th St.	760 3d Ave.—160 E. 47th St.
Fifty-third St.	3d Ave. and 53d St.	874 3d Ave.—164 E. 53d St.
Fifty-ninth St.*	3d Ave. and 59th St.	990 3d Ave.—164 E. 59th St.
Sixty-seventh St.	3d Ave. and 67th St.	1146 3d Ave.—168 E. 67th St.
Seventy-sixth St.	3d Ave. and 76th St.	1330 3d Ave.—200 E. 76th St.
Eighty-fourth St.	3d Ave. and 84th St.	1490 3d Ave.—173 E. 84th St.
Eighty-ninth St.	3d Ave. and 89th St.	1588 3d Ave.—169 E. 89th St.
Ninety-eighth St.	3d Ave. and 98th St.	1785 3d Ave.—158 E. 98th St.
106th Street.	3d Ave. and 106th St.	1925 3d Ave.—171 E. 106th St.
116th Street.	3d Ave. and 116th St.	2123 3d Ave.—184 E. 116th St.
125th Street.*	3d Ave. and 125th St.	2300 3d Ave.—192 E. 125th St.
129th Street.	3d Ave. and 129th St.	2380 3d Ave.—168 E. 129th St.

* Crosstown car lines.

Sixth Avenue Line.—(Daily, including Sundays.)

ROUTE.—Commencing at South Ferry, through Battery Park and Greenwich Street to Morris Street, thence through Trinity Place and Church Street, to Murray Street, to West Broadway and South 5th Avenue, to West Third Street, to 6th Avenue, to 58th Street. Harlem trains run through 53d Street to 9th Avenue, to 110th Street, to 8th Avenue, to 155th Street. Total distance, South Ferry to 155th St. and 8th Ave., 10.76 miles. South Ferry to 58th St. and 6th Ave., 5.18 miles. 50th St. to 58th St. and 6th Ave., 0.40 miles. Heaviest grade, 79 feet per mile. This line is open at all hours of the day and

night, including Sundays. Passengers for Grand Central Depot leave
train at 42d Street Station. Crosstown cars run between Station and
Depot. Fare 5 cents. 155th and 53d Street trains may be known by
green or red signals by day, and green or red lights by night, carried
on the forward part of the engine. All trains not displaying the
above, run to 58th Street (Central Park).

New York and Northern Railway Connection.—Trains connecting
with the New York and Northern Railway through trains carry a blue
disk on the forward part of the engine. Passengers for stations on
9th Avenue Line change cars at 59th Street Station. No extra
charge.

STATIONS.

NAME.	LOCATION.	NUMBERS AT INTERSECTION.
South Ferry.	Foot Whitehall St.	66 Whitehall—1 South St.
Battery Place.	Battery Pl. & Gr'nwich St.	1 Broadway.
Rector St.	New Church & Rector Sts.	71 Broadway.
Cortlandt St.	N. Church & Cortlandt Sts.	171 Broadway—25 Church St.
Park Place.	Church Street & Park Pl.	237 Broadway—40 Church St.
Chambers St.*	Hudson & Chambers Sts.	271 Broadway—1 Hudson St.
Franklin St.	W. B'way & Franklin Sts.	362 Broadway—125 Franklin.
Grand St.*	S. 5th Ave. and Grand St.	458 Broadway—52 Grand St.
Bleecker St.*	S. 5th Ave. & Bleecker St.	640 Broadway—139 Bleecker.
Eighth St.*	6th Ave. and 8th St.	100 6th Ave.—94 8th St.
Fourteenth St.*	6th Ave. and 14th St.	210 6th Ave.—65 W. 14th St.
Eighteenth St.	6th Ave. and 18th St.	286 6th Ave.—69 W. 18th St.
Twenty-third St.*	6th Ave. and 23d St.	375 6th Ave.—79 W. 23d St.
Twenty-eighth St.	6th Ave. and 28th St.	462 6th Ave.—59 W. 28th St.
Thirty-third St.*	6th Ave. and 33d St.	1280 Broadway—533 6th Ave.
Forty-second St.*	6th Ave. and 42d St.	736 6th Ave.—61 W. 42d St.
Fiftieth St.	6th Ave. and 50th St.	888 6th Ave.—81 W. 50th St.
Fifty-eighth St.	6th Ave. and 58th St.	1045 6th Ave —47 W. 58th St.
Fifty-third St.	8th Ave. and 53d St.	890 8th Ave.—247 W. 53d St.
Fifty-ninth St.*	9th Ave. and 59th St.	920 9th Ave.—357 W. 59th St.
Seventy-second St.	9th Ave. and 72d St.	1183 9th Ave.—101 W. 72d St.
Eighty-first St.	9th Ave. and 81st St.	1357 9th Ave.—100 W. 81st St.
Ninety-third St.	9th Ave. and 93d St.	1595 9th Ave.—102 W. 93d St.
104th Street.	9th Ave. and 104th St.	1821 9th Ave.—101 W. 104th St.
116th Street.	8th Ave. and 116th St.	2151 8th Ave.—301 W. 116th St.
125th Street.*	8th Ave. and 125th St.	2325 8th Ave.—300 W. 125th St.
135th Street.	8th Ave. and 135th St.	2525 8th Ave.
145th Street.	8th Ave. and 145th St.	....300 W. 145th St.
155th Street.	8th Ave. and 155th St.	Connecting with N. Y. & N. R'way for High Bridge, Brewster's, etc.

* Crosstown car lines.

Ninth Avenue Line.—(Daily, including Sundays.)

ROUTE.—Commencing at South Ferry, through Battery Park to Greenwich Street, to 9th Avenue, to 59th Street. Total distance, 5.08 miles. Heaviest grade, 107 feet per mile. This line is open from 5.30 A.M. to 7.57 P.M. Last train from 59th Street, South Bound, 7.57 P.M. Last train from South Ferry, North Bound, 8.21 P.M. Passengers for 72d St., 81st St., 93d St., 104th St., 116th St., 125th St. (Harlem), 135th St., 145th St., 155th St., Fort Washington, High Bridge, and the New York and Northern Railway, change cars at 59th St. No extra charge.

STATIONS.

NAME.	LOCATION.	NUMBERS AT INTERSECTION.
South Ferry.	Foot Whitehall St.	66 Whitehall—1 South St.
Battery Place.	Battery Pl. & Greenwich St.	1 Broadway.
Rector St.	Greenwich & Rector Sts.	71 Broadway—89 Greenwich.
Cortlandt St.	Gr'nwich & Cortlandt Sts.	171 Broadway—171 Greenwich.
Barclay St.	Greenwich & Barclay Sts.	227 Broadway—229 Greenwich.
Warren St.	Greenwich & Warren Sts.	259 Broadway—283 Greenwich.
Franklin St.	Greenwich & Franklin Sts.	362 Broadway—365 Greenwich.
Desbrosses St.*	Gr'nwich & Desbrosses Sts.	416 Broadway—452 Greenwich.
Houston St.*	Greenwich & Houston Sts.	300 W. H'ston—585 Greenwich.
Christopher St.*	Greenwich & Christo'r Sts.	146 Christop'r—680 Greenwich.
Fourteenth St.*	9th Ave. and 14th St.	59 9th Ave.—400 W. 14th St.
Twenty-third St.*	9th Ave. and 23d St.	212 9th Ave.—373 W. 23d St.
Thirtieth St.	9th Ave. and 30th St.	350 9th Ave.—367 W. 30th St.
Thirty-fourth St.*	9th Ave. and 34th St.	428 9th Ave.—365 W. 34th St.
Forty-second St.*	9th Ave. and 42d St.	580 9th Ave.—365 W. 42d St.
Fiftieth St.	9th Ave. and 50th St.	740 9th Ave.—371 W. 50th St.
Fifty-ninth St.*	9th Ave. and 59th St.	920 9th Ave.—357 W. 59th St.

* Crosstown car lines.

General Offices Manhattan Railway Co., No. 71 Broadway.

Rates of fare.—Five cents at all hours. Children under 5 years, free.

☞ Passengers are required to deposit their tickets in the Gate Box before entering train.

Points of Interest and how to Reach them by the Elevated Railways.

NAME.	LOCATION.	STATION AND LINE NEAREST.
Amberg's Germania Theatre,	15th Street and Irving Place,	14th Street—All Lines.
American Museum of Natural History,	8th Avenue and 79th Street,	81st Street—6th Avenue.
Astor House,	Broadway and Vesey Street,	Park Place—6th Avenue ; Barclay — 9th Avenue ; City Hall—2d and Third Avenues.
Academy of Music,	14th Street and Irving Place,	14th Street—All Lines.
Armory 7th Regiment,	66th Street and Lexington Avenue,	67th Street—3d Avenue ; 65th Street—2d Avenue.
Armory 12th Regiment,	61st Street and 9th Avenue,	59th Street—6th and 9th Avenues,
Armory 22d Regiment,	Boulevard and 67th Street.	72d Street — 6th and 9th Avenues.
Astor Library,	34 Lafayette Place,	8th Street—6th Avenue ; 9th Street—3d Avenue.
Academy of Design,	23d Street and 4th Avenue,	23d Street—All Lines.
Albemarle Hotel,	24th Street and Broadway,	23d Street—All Lines.
Arsenal,	35th Street and 7th Avenue,	33d Street—6th Avenue ; 34th Street—2d, 3d, and 9th Avenues.
American Institute,	63d Street and 3d Avenue,	67th Street—3d Avenue ; 65th Street—2d Avenue.
Anchor Line Steamers,	Foot Le Roy Street for Glasgow,	Houston—3d and 9th Avenues ; 8th Street — 6th Avenue.
Albany Day Line,	Foot Vestry Street, North River,	Desbrosses—9th Avenue ; Grand Street—2d, 3d, and 6th Avenues.
Astoria Ferry,	Foot 92d Street, East River,	92d Street—2d Avenue ; 89th Street—3d Avenue.

NAME.	LOCATION.	STATION AND LINE NEAREST.
Atlanta Casino,	155th Street and 8th Avenue,	155th Street—6th Avenue.
Barge Office— Government,	Battery Park,	South Ferry—All Lines.
Bartholdi Statue,	New York Bay,	South Ferry—All Lines.
Blackwell's Island Ferry,	52d Street, East River,	50th Street—2d Avenue ; 53d Street—3d Avenue.
Bay Ridge Ferry,	Whitehall Street, East River,	South Ferry—All Lines.
Battery Park,	Foot Broadway,	South Ferry, or Battery Place—All Lines.
Barrett House,	43d Street and Broadway,	42d Street—All Lines.
Brooklyn Bridge,	City Hall Park,	City Hall—2d and 3d Avenues ; Park Place—6th Avenue ; Warren — 9th Avenue.
Bible House,	8th Street and 4th Avenue,	8th Street—6th Avenue ; 9th Street—3d Avenue.
Bellevue Hospital,	Foot East 26th Street,	23d Street—All Lines.
Bryant Park,	42d Street and 6th Avenue,	42d Street—All Lines.
Brunswick Hotel,	26th Street and 5th Avenue,	28th Street—3d and 6th Avenues.
Brevoort House,	8th Street and 5th Avenue,	8th Street—6th Avenue ; 9th Street—3d Avenue.
Bloomingdale Insane Asylum,	Boulevard and West 117th Street,	116th Street—6th and 3d Avenues.
Buckingham Hotel,	50th Street and 5th Avenue,	50th Street—6th Avenue ; 47th Street—3d Avenue.
Broadway Theatre,	41st Street and Broadway,	42d Street—All Lines.
Bristol Hotel,	42d Street and 5th Avenue.	42d Street—All Lines.
Base Ball Grounds,	155th Street and 8th Avenue	155th Street—6th and 9th Avenues.

NAME.	LOCATION.	STATION AND LINE NEAREST.
Blind Asylum,	34th Street and 9th Avenue,	34th Street—2d, 3d, and 9th Avenues ; 33d Street —6th Avenue.
Bijou Opera House,	30th Street and Broadway,	8th Street—3d and 6th Avenues.
Bremen Line,	2d Street, Hoboken,	See Hoboken and Christopher Street Ferries.
Castle Garden,	Battery Park, North River,	South Ferry, or Battery Place—All Lines.
Custom House,	Wall and William Streets,	Rector—6th and 9th Avenues ; Hanover Square— 2d and 3d Avenues.
Cotton Exchange,	Hanover Square,	Rector—6th and 9th Avenues ; Hanover Square— 2d and 3d Avenues.
Coleman House,	27th Street and Broadway,	28th Street—3d and 6th Avenues.
City Buildings,	City Hall Park,	City Hall—2d and 3d Avenues ; Park Place—6th Avenue ; Warren — 9th Avenue.
Cooper Institute,	Junction 3d and 4th Avenues,	8th Street—6th Avenue ; 9th Street—3d Avenue.
College Physicians and Surgeons,	437 West 59th Street,	59th Street—6th and 9th Avenues.
Clarendon Hotel,	18th Street and Union Square,	18th Street—3d and 6th Avenues.
Cosmopolitan Hotel,	Chambers Street and West Broadway,	Chambers — 6th Avenue ; City Hall—2d and 3d Avenues ; Warren—9th Avenue.
College City of New York,	23d Street and Lexington Avenue,	23d Street—All Lines.
College Point Ferry,	Foot 99th Street, East River,	92d Street—2d Avenue ; 99th Street—3d Avenue.
Convent Sacred Heart,	St. Nicholas Avenue, above 126th,	125th Street—3d and 6th Avenues.

NAME.	LOCATION.	STATION AND LINE NEAREST.
Columbia College,	49th Street and Madison Avenue,	50th Street—6th Avenue ; 47th Street—3d Avenue.
Central Railroad of New Jersey,	Foot Liberty Street, North River,	Cortlandt—6th and 9th Avenues ; Fulton—2d and 3d Avenues.
Cunard Line Steamers,	Foot Clarkson Street, North River,	Houston—9th and 3d Avenues ; Bleecker — 6th Avenue.
Catharine Ferry,	Foot Catharine Street, East River,	Chatham Square—2d and 3d Avenues.
Christopher Street Ferry,	Foot Christopher Street, North River,	Christopher—9th Avenue ; 8th Street—2d and 6th Avenues ; 9th Street— 3d Avenue.
Catharine Market,	Catharine and South Streets,	Chatham Square—2d and 3d Avenues.
Central Park, {	Lower Entrance, {	59th Street—3d, 6th, and 9th Avenues. 58th Street—6th Avenue.
	Central Entrance, East Side,	84th Street—3d Avenue ; 80th Street—2d Avenue.
	Central Entrance, West Side,	81st Street—6th Avenue.
	Upper Entrance,	106th Street—3d Avenue ; 116th Street—6th Avenue.
Casino,	39th Street and Broadway,	42d Street—All Lines.
Chickering Hall,	5th Avenue and 18th Street,	18th Street—3d and 6th Avenues.
College of Pharmacy,	115 West 68th Street,	72d Street—6th and 9th Avenues.
Cancer Hospital,	105th Street and 8th Avenue,	104th Street—6th Avenue.
Children's Aid Society,	4th Street and Lafayette Place,	9th Street — 3d Avenue ; 8th Street—6th Avenue.
Citizen's Line,	Foot Christopher Street, North River,	9th Street — 3d Avenue ; 8th Street—2d and 6th Avenues ; Christopher— 9th Avenue.

NAME.	LOCATION.	STATION AND LINE NEAREST
Dam Hotel,	Union Square and 15th Street,	14th Street—All Lines.
Dental College,	2d Avenue and 23d Street,	23d Street—All Lines.
Delmonico's,	26th Street and Broadway,	28th Street—3d and 6th Avenues.
Deaf and Dumb Asylum,	162d Street and Boulevard,	155th Street—6th Avenue.
Delaware, Lackawanna and Western Railroad,	Foot Barclay Street, North River,	Barclay—9th Avenue ; Park Place—6th Avenue ; City Hall—2d and 3d Avenues.
	Foot Christopher Street, North River,	Christopher—9th Avenue ; 8th Street—2d and 6th Avenues ; 9th Street—3d Avenue.
Daly's Theatre,	30th Street and Broadway,	28th Street—3d and 6th Avenues.
Everett House,	17th Street and Union Square,	18th Street—3d and 6th Avenues.
East River Park,	84th Street and East River,	86th Street—2d Avenue ; 84th Street—3d Avenue.
Eden Musée,	23d Street, between 5th and 6th Avenues,	23d Street—All Lines.
Fulton Market,	Fulton and South Streets,	Fulton—2d and 3d Avenues ; Cortlandt—6th and 9th Avenues.
Fifth Avenue Hotel,	23d Street and Broadway,	23d Street—All Lines.
Foundling Asylum,	68th Street and Lexington Avenue,	67th Street—3d Avenue ; 65th Street—2d Avenue.

NAME.	LOCATION.	STATION AND LINE NEAREST.
Fall River Steamers,	Foot Murray Street, North River,	Park Place—6th Avenue ; Warren — 9th Avenue ; City Hall—2d and 3d Avenues.
Fulton Ferry,	Foot Fulton Street, East River,	Fulton—2d and 3d Avenues ; Cortlandt—6th and 9th Avenues.
Fifth Avenue Theatre,	28th Street and Broadway,	28th Street—3d and 6th Avenues.
French Line,	Morton Street, North River,	Houston—3d and 9th Avenues ; Bleecker—6th Avenue.
Fourteenth Street Theatre,	14th Street and 6th Avenue,	14th Street—All Lines.
Governor's Island,	New York Bay,	South Ferry—All Lines.
Grand Street Ferry,	Foot Grand Street, East River,	Grand—2d, 3d, and 6th Avenues.
Greenpoint Ferry,	Foot 23d Street, East River,	23d Street—All Lines.
Gilsey House,	29th Street and Broadway,	28th Street—3d and 6th Avenues.
Gansevoort Market,	Foot Gansevoort Street,	14th Street—All Lines.
Grand Central Hotel,	Broadway, above Bleecker Street,	Houston—3d and 9th Avenues ; Bleecker—6th Avenue.
Grand Central Station,	42d Street and 4th Avenue,	42d Street—All Lines.
GRAND UNION HOTEL,	4th Avenue and 42d Street,	42d Street—All Lines.
German Hospital,	77th Street and 4th Avenue,	76th Street—3d Avenue ; 75th Street—2d Avenue.
Grand Opera House,	8th Avenue and 23d Street,	23d Street—All Lines.
Gramercy Park,	21st Street and Lexington Avenue,	23d Street—All Lines.

NAME.	LOCATION.	STATION AND LINE NEAREST.
Grand Hotel,	31st Street and Broadway,	33d Street—6th Avenue; 28th Street—3d Avenue.
Gedney House,	40th Street and Broadway,	42d Street—All Lines.
Hamilton Ferry,	Foot Whitehall Street,	South Ferry—All Lines.
Hunter's Point Ferry,	Foot 34th Street, East River,	34th Street Ferry—2d and 3d Avenues.
Hoboken Ferry,	Foot Barclay Street, North River,	Barclay—9th Avenue; Park Place—6th Avenue; City Hall—2d and 3d Avenues.
Harlem River Park,	126th Street and 2d Avenue,	127th Street—2d Avenue; 125th Street—3d and 6th Avenues.
Hoffman House,	25th Street and Broadway,	23d Street—All Lines.
Homeopathic Medical College,	Avenue A and East 63d Street.	65th Street—2d Avenue.
Homeopathic Hospital,	4th Avenue and 67th Street,	65th Street—2d Avenue, 67th Street—3d Avenue.
Harlem Railroad, **Hudson River Railroad,**	42d Street and 4th Avenue,	All Lines.
Havana Line, **Ward's,**	Pier 16, East River,	Hanover Square—2d and 3d Avenues.
Houston Street Ferry,	Foot Houston Street, East River,	1st Street—2d Avenue; Bleecker—6th Avenue; Houston—3d and 9th Avenues.

NAME.	LOCATION.	STATION AND LINE NEAREST.
Hamburg Packet Line,	Foot 1st Street, Hoboken,	See Hoboken and Christopher Street Ferries.
Home for Aged and Infirm Hebrews,	105th Street and 9th Avenue,	104th Street—6th Avenue.
Imperial German Mail,	2d and 3d Streets, Hoboken,	See Hoboken and Christopher Street Ferries.
Iron Steamboat Line,	Pier 1, North River,	South Ferry, or Battery Place—All Lines.
Jones' Woods,	68th Street and Avenue A,	67th Street—3d Avenue ; 70th Street—2d Avenue.
Jefferson Market,	9th Street and 6th Avenue,	8th Street—6th Avenue ; 9th Street—3d Avenue.
Juvenile Asylum,	176th Street and 10th Avenue,	155th Street—6th Avenue.
Jersey City Ferry,	Foot Cortlandt Street, North River,	Cortlandt—6th and 9th Avenues ; Fulton—2d and 3d Avenues.
	Foot Desbrosses Street, North River,	Desbrosses—9th Avenue ; Grand—2d, 3d, and 6th Avenues.
Koster and Bial's,	34th Street near Broadway,	33d Street—6th Avenue.
Lion Park,	110th Street and 9th Avenue.	104th Street—6th Avenue ; 106th Street—3d Avenue.
Long Island Railroad,	Foot 34th Street, East River.	34th Street Ferry—2d and 3d Avenues.
Lehigh Valley Railroad,	See Pennsylvania Railroad,	
Lyceum Theatre,	23d Street and 4th Avenue,	23d Street—All Lines.

NAME.	LOCATION.	STATION AND LINE NEAREST.
Manhattan Beach,	Foot Whitehall Street,	South Ferry—All lines.
Manhattan Square Park,	77th and 81st Streets, 8th and 9th Avenues,	81st Street—6th Avenue ; 84th Street—3d Avenue.
Marlborough Hotel,	Broadway and 36th Street,	33d Street—6th Avenue ; 34th Street—2d, 3d, and 9th Avenues.
Metropole Hotel,	42d Street and Broadway,	42d Street—All Lines.
Metropolitan Museum of Art,	Central Park,	84th Street—3d Avenue ; 81st Street—6th Avenue.
Mercantile Library,	Astor Place and 8th Street,	9th Street—3d Avenue ; 8th Street—6th Avenue.
Metropolitan Opera House,	39th Street and Broadway,	42d Street—All Lines.
Madison Square Park,	23d Street and Broadway,	23d Street—All Lines.
Morningside Park,	8th Avenue and 110th Street,	104th Street—6th Avenue ; 106th Street—3d Avenue.
Madison Square Theatre,	4 West 24th Street,	23d Street—All Lines.
Madison Square Garden,	26th Street and Madison Avenue,	28th Street—3d and 6th Avenues.
Medical University,	Foot East 26th Street,	28th Street—3d and 6th Avenues.
Manhattan College,	West 131st Street and Boulevard.	125th Street—3d and 6th Avenues.
Masonic Temple,	23d Street and 6th Avenue,	23d Street—All Lines.
Mount Sinai Hospital,	66th Street and Lexington Avenue,	65th Street—2d Avenue ; 67th Street—3d Avenue.
Mount Morris Park,	5th Avenue and 124th Street,	125th Street—3d and 6th Avenues.

NAME.	LOCATION.	STATION AND LINE NEAREST.
Monarch Line,	Pavonia Ferry, Jersey City,	See N. Y., L. E. & W. R. R.
Morton House,	14th Street and Broadway,	14th Street—All Lines.
Montefiore Home for Chronic Invalids,	84th Street and Avenue A,	84th Street—3d Avenue ; 86th Street—2d Avenue.
Manhattan Athletic Grounds,	8th Avenue and 86th Street,	81st Street—6th Avenue ; 84th Street—3d Avenue.
Murray Hill Hotel,	40th Street and Park Avenue,	42d Street—All Lines.
Normandie Hotel,	38th Street and Broadway,	42d Street—All Lines.
New York Hospital,	15th Street and 5th Avenue,	14th Street—All Lines.
Niblo's Garden,	Prince Street and Broadway,	Bleecker—6th Avenue ; Houston—3d and 9th Avenues.
New York Central and Hudson River Railroad,	42d Street and 4th Avenue,	42d Street—All Lines.
New York, Lake Erie and Western Railroad,	Foot Chambers Street, North River, Foot 23d Street, North River,	Chambers—6th Avenue ; Warren—9th Ave. ; City Hall—2d and 3d Avenues. 23d Street—All Lines.
West Shore Railroad,	Jay and 42d Streets, North River,	Franklin—6th and 9th Avenues ; 42d Street—All Lines.
New York and Northern Railway,	155th Street and 8th Avenue,	155th Street—6th Avenue.

NAME.	LOCATION.	STATION AND LINE NEAREST.
New Jersey Southern Railroad,	Foot Rector Street, North River,	Rector—6th and 9th Avenues; Hanover Square—2d and 3d Avenues.
New York and New Haven Railroad,	42d Street and 4th Avenue,	42d Street—All Lines.
Normal College,	67th Street and Lexington Avenue,	65th Street—2d Avenue; 67th Street—3d Avenue.
Norwich Line,	Pier 40, North River, Watts Street,	Desbrosses—9th Avenue; Grand—2d, 3d, and 6th Avenues.
National Line Steamships,	Houston Street, North River,	Houston—3d and 9th Avenues; Bleecker—6th Avenue.
Ophthalmic Hospital,	23d Street and 3d Avenue,	23d Street—All Lines.
Obelisk,	Central Park,	84th Street—3d Avenue; 81st Street—6th Avenue.
Orphan Asylum,	74th Street and Bloomingdale Road,	72d Street—6th Avenue.
People's Theatre,	Prince Street and Bowery,	Houston—3d Avenue; Bleecker—6th Avenue.
Pastor's Theatre,	14th Street, near 3d Avenue,	14th Street—All Lines.
Produce Exchange,	Whitehall and Beaver Streets.	South Ferry—All Lines; or Battery Place—6th and 9th Avenues.
Post-Office,	Broadway and Park Row,	City Hall—2d and 3d Avenues; Park Place—6th Avenue; Barclay—9th Avenue.

NAME.	LOCATION.	STATION AND LINE NEAREST.
Printing House Square,	Spruce and Nassau Streets,	City Hall—2d and 3d Avenues ; Park Place—6th Avenue ; Barclay—9th Avenue.
Polo Grounds,	155th Street and 8th Avenue.	155th Street—6th and 9th Avenues.
Pavonia Ferry,	Foot Chambers Street, North River,	Warren—9th Avenue ; Chamber Street—6 t h Avenue ; City Hall—2d and 3d Avenues.
Pennsylvania Railroad,	Foot Cortlandt Street, North River,	Cortlandt—6th and 9th Avenues; Fulton—2d and 3d Avenues.
	Foot Desbrosses Street, North River,	Desbrosses—9th Avenue ; Grand—2d, 3d, and 6th Avenues.
Park Theatre,	35th Street and Broadway,	33d St.—6th Avenue ; 34th Street—2d, 3d, and 9th Avenues.
Palmer's Theatre	30th Street and Broadway,	28th Street—3d and 6th Avenues.
People's Line,	Foot Canal Street, North River,	Desbrosses—9th Avenue ; Grand—2d, 3d, and 6th Avenues.
Pacific Mail Steamers,	Foot Canal Street North River,	Desbrosses—9th Avenue ; Grand—2d, 3d, and 6th Avenues.
Providence Line,	Foot Warren Street, North River,	Warren—9th Avenue ; City Hall—2d and 3d Avenues; Chambers Street—6th Avenue.
Park Avenue Hotel,	33d Street and Park Avenue,	33d Street—6th Avenue ; 34th Street—2d, 3d, and 9th Avenues.
Presbyterian Hospital,	4th Avenue and 70th Street,	67th Street—3d Avenue ; 70th Street—2d Avenue.
Parepa Hall,	86th Street and 3d Avenue	86th Street—2d Avenue ; 84th Street—3d Avenue.
Plaza Hotel,	5th Avenue and 59th Street,	58th Street—6th Avenue ; 59th Street—3d Avenue.

NAME.	LOCATION.	STATION AND LINE NEAREST.
Red Star Line,	Grand Street, Jersey City,	See Pennsylvania Railroad.
Roosevelt Street Ferry,	Foot Roosevelt Street, East River,	Franklin Square—2d and 3d Avenues.
Riverside Park,	72d Street and Hudson River,	72d Street—6th Avenue ; 125th Street—3d and 6th Avenues.
Roosevelt Hospital,	59th Street and 9th Avenue,	59th Street—3d, 6th and 9th Avenues.
St. Vincent Hospital,	11th Street and Greenwich Avenue,	9th Street—3d Avenue ; Christopher—9th Avenue ; 8th Street—2d and 6th Avenues.
Steinway Hall,	14th Street and Union Square,	14th Street—All Lines.
Staten Island Ferry,	Foot Whitehall Street,	South Ferry—All Lines.
South Ferry,	Foot Whitehall Street,	South Ferry—All Lines.
Scottish Rite Hall,	29th Street and Madison Avenue,	28th Street—3d and 6th Avenues.
Stock Exchange,	Broad and Wall Streets,	Rector—6th and 9th Avenues ; Hanover Square—2d and 3d Avenues.
Stock Exchange Consolidated,	Broadway and Exchange Place,	Rector—6th and 9th Avenues ; Hanover Square—2d and 3d Avenues.
St. James Hotel,	26th Street and Broadway,	28th Street—3d and 6th Avenues.
Sturtevant House	28th Street and Broadway,	28th Street—3d and 6th Avenues.
St. Luke's Hospital,	54th Street and 5th Avenue,	50th Street—2d, 6th and 9th Avenues ; 53d Street —3d Avenue.

Name.	Location.	Station and Line Nearest.
St. Patrick's Cathedral,	51st Street and 5th Avenue,	50th Street—2d, 6th and 9th Avenues ; 53d Street —3d Avenue.
St. Paul's Church,	Vesey Street and Broadway,	Park Place—6th Avenue ; Barclay Street—9th Avenue ; City Hall—2d and 3d Avenues.
Stonington Line,	Foot Spring Street, North River,	Grand—2d, 3d and 6th Avenues ; Desbrosses—· 9th Avenue.
State Line Steamers,	Foot Canal Street, North River,	Desbrosses—9th Avenue ; Grand—2d, 3d and 6th Avenues.
Savannah Steamers,	Foot Spring Street, North River,	Desbrosses—9th Avenue ; Grand—2d, 3d and 6th Avenues.
Stuyvesant Square,	15th Street and Stuyvesant Place,	14th Street—All Lines.
St. Cloud Hotel,	42d Street and Broadway,	42d Street—All Lines.
St. Denis Hotel,	11th Street and Broadway,	14th Street—6th Avenue ; 9th Street—3d Avenue.
Stevens House,	Broadway and Morris Street,	Rector—6th and 9th Avenues.
Standard Theatre,	33d Street and Broadway,	33d Street—6th Avenue ; 34th Street—2d, 3d and 9th Avenues.
Star Theatre,	13th Street and Broadway,	14th Street—All Lines.
Theatre Comique	125th Street and 3d Avenue.	125th Street—3d and 6th Avenues.
Thalia Theatre,	Canal Street and Bowery,	Canal—2d and 3d Avenues ; Grand—6th Avenue.
Tammany Hall,	14th Street, near 3d Avenue,	14th Street—All Lines.
Trinity Church,	Broadway and Rector Street,	Rector—6th and 9th Avenues ; Hanover Square— 2d and 3d Avenues.

NAME.	LOCATION.	STATION AND LINE NEAREST.
Trinity Cemetery	155th Street and 10th Avenue,	155th Street—6th Avenue.
Tompkins Square,	East 7th Street and Avenue A,	8th Street—2d Avenue ; 9th Street—3d Avenue.
Theiss' Music Hall,	14th Street, near 3d Avenue,	14th Street—All Lines.
Tomb of General Grant,	122d Street and Riverside Park,	125th Street—3d and 6th Avenues.
Thirty-ninth Street Brooklyn Ferry,	Foot Whitehall Street,	South Ferry—All Lines.
Twenty-third street Brooklyn Ferry,	Foot 23d Street, East River,	23d Street—All Lines.
Union Square,	14th Street and Broadway,	14th Street—All Lines.
Union League Club,	37th Street and 5th Avenue,	33d Street—6th Avenue ; 34th Street—2d, 3d and 9th Avenues.
United States Sub-Treasury,	Wall and Nassau Streets,	Rector—6th and 9th Avenues ; Hanover Square— 2d and 3d Avenues.
United States Signal Service Bureau,	120 Broadway,	Rector—6th and 9th Avenues ; Hanover Square— 2d and 3d Avenues.
Union Square Theatre,	14th Street and Union Square,	14th Street—All Lines.
Union Square Hotel,	15th Street and Union Square,	14th Street—All Lines.
Vendome Hotel,	41st Street and Broadway,	42d Street—All Lines.
Victoria Hotel,	27th Street and Broadway,	28th Street—3d and 6th Avenues.

NAME.	LOCATION.	STATION AND LINE NEAREST.
Ward's Island Ferry,	110th Street and East River,	111th Street—2d Avenue ; 106th Street—3d Avenue.
Westminster Hotel,	Irving Place and 16th Street,	14th Street—All Lines.
Wall Street Ferry,	Foot Wall Street, East River,	Hanover Square—2d and 3d Avenues ; Rector—6th and 9th Avenues.
Williamsburg Ferry,	Foot Grand Street, East River,	Grand—2d, 3d and 6th Avenues.
Weehawken Ferry,	Foot 42d Street, North River,	42d Street—All Lines.
	Foot Jay Street, North River,	Franklin—6th and 9th Avenues.
Washington Market,	Vesey and Washington Streets,	Barclay—9th Avenue ; Park Place—6th Avenue ; City Hall—2d and 3d Avenues.
Windsor Hotel,	5th Avenue and 47th Street,	50th Street—6th and 9th Avenues ; 47th Street—3d Avenue.
Washington Square,	5th Avenue and Waverly Place,	8th Street—6th Avenue ; 9th Street—3d Avenue.
White Star Line,	Foot West 10th Street, North River,	Christopher—9th Avenue ; 8th Street—6th Avenue.
Young Men's Christian Association,	23d Street and 4th Avenue,	23d Street—All Lines.
Young Women's Christian Association,	7 East 15th Street,	18th Street—3d and 6th Avenues.

MORE THAN

150,000 PEOPLE

STOPPED AT THE

GRAND UNION HOTEL

DURING THE PAST YEAR.

ITS POPULARITY

is mainly due to the following facts:

The policy of its proprietors is to please guests.

Its rooms are well furnished and scrupulously clean, and range in price from $1 (for an excellent room) up to $3 and $4 per day.

The food is of the best quality obtainable, well cooked, the prices are moderate, and the portions liberal.

It is centrally located. Elevated railroads and street cars to all parts of the city pass its doors.

It is immediately opposite the Grand Central Depot, to and from which guests' baggage is delivered free.

Its volume of business is such that more value can be given for the money than at any other first-class hotel in the city.

FORD & CO.,
Proprietors.

INDEX.

134